The Luck Runs Out

CHARLOTTE MACLEOD

 AVON
PUBLISHERS OF BARD, CAMELOT, DISCUS AND FLARE BOOKS

AVON BOOKS
A division of
The Hearst Corporation
1790 Broadway
New York, New York 10019

Copyright © 1979 by Charlotte MacLeod
Published by arrangement with Doubleday & Company, Inc.
Library of Congress Catalog Card Number: 79-7606
ISBN: 0-380-54171-8

First Avon Printing, March, 1981

AVON TRADEMARK REG. U.S. PAT. OFF. AND IN
OTHER COUNTRIES, MARCA REGISTRADA,
HECHO EN CANADA

Printed in Canada

UNV 10 9 8 7

For Betty and Arnold

Chapter 1

"My stars and garters, Odin, I don't see how any horse alive can wear out shoes the way you do."

Clucking like a mother hen, the farrier settled the enormous Balaclava Black's massive hoof cozily into the lap of her leather apron, picked up a sharp, short-bladed knife, and began paring at the edges with deft, quick flicks. Helen Shandy, who had been Helen Marsh until a couple of months ago, stood as close as she dared, watching. She was still trying to learn her way around the sprawling complex of Balaclava Agricultural College, and the animal husbandry barns were her current field of investigation. So far, her most intriguing discovery was Flackley the Farrier.

Helen herself was petite, fair, fortyish, and daintily rounded. Miss Flackley was even smaller, pushing sixty, and not rounded at all, as far as external evidence could indicate. If she hadn't been giving a draft horse a pedicure, Mrs. Shandy would never have guessed her profession.

The farrier had on neat brown corduroy pants and jacket. Her shoes were polished brown oxfords about size four and a half. Her grizzled hair was tucked up into a dashing tam o'shanter crocheted of ombre worsted in shades of tan and rust. A harmonizing scarf was tucked into the neck of her spotless beige flannel shirt. Her hands were protected by yellow cotton gardening gloves and her face by a discreet film of cold cream. Nothing about her was out of place except the gold-rimmed bifocals that slid down her tiny nose as she exchanged the knife for a file as long as her forearm and began to smooth the hoof she'd trimmed.

"He looks as if he's loving it," Helen observed.

"Yes, Odin does enjoy being fussed over," Miss Flackley agreed. "They all do, except Loki. He's a very private horse."

" 'I pay respect to wisdom, not to strength,' " Helen murmured.

"That's C. S. Lewis, isn't it?" Miss Flackley surprised her by saying. "Yes, Loki does have that thoughtful, melancholy streak in him. I suppose it comes from being the littlest."

Helen glanced along the row of eight stalls, each with its occupant's name carved on a solid walnut quarterboard above, each with one of the horse's iron shoes mounted on the lower half of the divided door. Loki's was in truth a fraction shorter than the rest. Even so, it looked tremendous to her.

"I wonder why they always hang them with the ends up," she mused. "I suppose it's some ancient superstition."

"It can't be so very ancient," replied the astonishing Miss Flackley. "Horseshoeing as we know it wasn't prevalent till the Middle Ages, though of course folks must have known long before then that the hooves of solid-ungulates tend to wear off at the edges once the poor beasts have to earn their oats by the sweat of their brows like the rest of us poor sinners here below. The old Romans used to put leather sandals on their horses, and the Japanese had 'em shuffling around in straw slippers. William the Conqueror's supposed to have brought horseshoeing to England from Europe, so it must have been common practice by the time we started colonizing America. Hold still, Odin."

She quieted the towering animal with a light pat on the flank.

"Doesn't hurt them any more than cutting your toenails if you go about it right. Where was I? Oh yes, about hanging horeshoes. There's been a good deal of controversy about that over the years, but the more enlightened modern opinion is that the points should be up. They always make me think of that Egyptian goddess with the horned headdress. Isis? Hathor? I never could keep'em straight. Anyway, I expect she had something to do with fertility."

"They generally did," said Helen, much interested.

"On the other hand," Miss Flackley went on, "if you turn a horseshoe upside down, you get the Greek Omega, the last letter in their alphabet, as I'm sure you know better than I. So there's life and growth one way and finality the other. If you think of death as finality, I suppose you might get to thinking points up is lucky and points down is unfavorable. Of course that's only my ignorant notion. Here's Professor Stott coming, and I'm sure he could give you a more sensible answer than I."

The chairman of the animal husbandry department was indeed bearing down upon them with stately step and slow. Professor Stott, knowing that haste made waste and took off valuable poundage, had in the ripeness of his manhood developed a girth and tranquillity unequaled except perhaps by the college's prize hog, Balthazar of Balaclava.

Stott and Balthazar had a great deal in common. With his well-fleshed frame, his healthy pink skin, his bright little blue eyes set deep into firm fat, and that benign expression which bespeaks equanimity of temperament combined with firmness of principle, Professor Stott would have made a remarkably handsome pig. Catching sight of Helen, whom he liked, and Miss Flackley, whom he respected, he drew to a halt and elevated his green porkpie hat.

"Good afternoon, ladies."

"Good afternoon, Professor," said the farrier. "Mrs. Shandy was just asking me why we hang horseshoes with their points up instead of down. Perhaps you could elucidate."

Hat in hand, the man of learning pondered. At last he issued his pronouncement:

"To keep the luck from running out."

"Well, there, now," said Miss Flackley. "That goes to show, if you want an intelligent answer, go straight to the expert. How's Belinda today, Professor?"

She was referring to Balthazar's latest consort, a beautiful young sow of whom Stott had great hopes. A slight shadow passed across the distinguished man's countenance.

"I was about to ask for your professional opinion, Miss Flackley. In general, Belinda appears well and happy, yet I fancy that I detect a certain vague discomfort after mash."

"Only to be expected, I should think," Miss Flackley replied. "After all, she's due to farrow soon. Become a mother, I should have said," she amended, turning to Helen with an air of apology. "Please forgive my rude, bucolic phraseology."

"You should hear my husband's when he gets going about organic fertilizers," Helen reassured her. "But I mustn't keep you chatting if Belinda's having pains in her tum."

"Won't you come with us, Mrs. Shandy? That sow is something to see, I can tell you."

"I'll say she is!" Professor Stott's tiny blue eyes sparkled, his lips curved in a smile that might almost have been termed boyish. "Come on, Mrs. Shandy, you must meet Belinda."

"I'd love to, but some people are coming to dinner and I haven't done a thing about it. Oh, Miss Flackley," she added on impulse, "could I coax you to dine with us some night soon? How about Friday?"

"Why"—the farrier put down her file and studied the professor's wife in surprise. There was no earthly reason why she should not be invited to break bread among the faculty, but evidently she'd never been asked to do so before. Perhaps she decided it was time. In any event, she nodded her neat head.

"I should be delighted, and Friday will suit me very well. At what time shall I come?"

"Would half-past six be convenient? It's the little brick house on the Crescent."

"I know." A slight smile flitted across Miss Flackley's unpainted lips. After his eccentric behavior during the Grand Illumination at Christmastime* there wasn't a soul around Balaclava Junction who didn't know where Peter Shandy lived. "Six-thirty is perfect."

"Good, then we'll expect you. Professor Stott, you come, too. I'll make you a noodle pudding. May I visit Belinda tomorrow, instead?"

---

* *Rest You Merry*, Doubleday Crime Club, 1978.

"Pleasure."

With that portmanteau word, Professor Stott put his hat on and set his bulk in motion toward the piggery. Miss Flackley followed a respectful three paces behind. Helen tucked the collar of her storm coat more snugly around her throat, for the April wind was still raw in Massachusetts, and hurried across the campus toward home.

She'd been having a series of little dinners lately. Naturally, some people got invited oftener than others. Tonight, they were having the Enderbles, an elderly couple whom everybody adored, and Timothy Ames, Peter's most valued friend and colleague. Tim also happened to be the father of Jemmy, who had married Dave Marsh, a young relative of Helen's. Coming to keep house for Tim after his wife had been found dead behind Peter's sofa, she had soon deserted Ames for Shandy. Because she still had slight guilt feelings and because she'd developed a fondness for the crusty old gnome, Helen was going all out to be kind to Tim and the housekeeper whom Jemmy had bullied her father into hiring after Helen married Peter.

Being kind to Tim's new housekeeper was a test of friendship. Professor Ames's late wife had been domineering, nosy, overtalkative, and generally obnoxious. Left to his own choosing, Ames had inevitably saddled himself with another woman of the same type. The chief difference was that while Jemima Ames had been the sloppiest housewife who ever cluttered a kitchen, Lorene McSpee was relentlessly, indefatigably, overwhelmingly clean.

In days past, the Ames house, which stood directly across the Crescent from Shandy's, had stunk of mildew, stale smoke, and unemptied trash baskets. Now it was impossible to stroll past the place without having one's sinuses blasted by wafts of ammonia. The neighbors tried to convince each other that this change was highly laudable. Tim was lucky to get such a good worker. Besides, it was hard to find anybody at all willing to live in, which was a must because Professor Ames was deaf and getting on in years. Everybody who had Tim's interests at heart must help him hang onto this paragon of prophylaxis. So Helen had invited Lorene McSpee, too.

They'd probably survive the evening. Mary Enderble could be counted on to keep up a merry prattle. After dinner Peter would probably lure the other men into the cubbyhole he called his office, where there was literally no room for the three women to fit. Well, in a pinch, she could always take Lorene to the kitchen and compare disinfectants.

Planning menus in her head, Helen mounted the not inconsiderable rise toward the residential area. Balaclava's campus was extensive, covering a series of hills and vales, and the animal husbandry buildings were quite properly situated at the lowest and farthest part, a good three-quarters of a mile from the administration building, classrooms, and dormitories. She got home winded but organized, hung up her coat and got straight to work. When Peter came in from his afternoon classes the table was set, drinks were out, the house filled with good smells. He sniffed with satisfaction.

"How wise I was to marry you. Chicken divan and gingerbread with applesauce, if I mistake not."

"When did you ever?" She gave him a kiss. "I thought I'd set a bucket of bleach water by Mrs. McSpee's place, to make her feel at home. Whatever happened to Mr. McSpee, I wonder."

"Ate him on the wedding night, I expect."

"No, I'd say she kept him in the bath with a gallon of Lysol. Peter, I don't really think I care for that woman."

"Therein you show excellent taste and keen discernment, my love. So why in tunket did you invite her to dinner?"

"Because Tim is your friend and Jemmy's father. It was the least I could do."

"The least you could do was not invite anybody. It is not in your nature to do the least you can do. I only wish you'd expend some of that ill-directed goodwill of yours finding Tim a decent woman instead of that raving ammoniac."

"He had one, but you were her undoing. Take your lecherous paws off me, you seducing hound!"

"You don't really mean that?"

"Actually I don't, but we haven't the time right now."

Helen refastened her blouse buttons. "To tell you the truth, Peter, I have done something. At least I've set the wheels in motion. Aren't you even going to wash your hands before the company comes?"

"My hands are clean," said her husband sternly, "and I hope I can say the same for yours. What wheels?"

"Well," said Helen, fiddling self-consciously with a pot-holder, "back when I was working in South Dakota, I had the dearest, sweetest, most absolutely precious—"

"Poodle? Lover? Goldfish?"

"Landlady. She was the sole surviving scion of an ancient family."

"Humbug!"

"She was so. Her grandfather on the paternal side had been a distinguished manufacturer of buggy whips and carriage robes. He built a palatial seven-room mansion in the Late American Gothic style."

"Did it have indoor plumbing?"

"Not exactly, but the chamber pots were tastefully decorated to match the slop bowls. Anyway, in the fullness of time, Iduna fell heir to the place. There wasn't much else for her to fall heir to, the buggy whip business having fallen on evil days, so Iduna ran it as a lodging house."

"Iduna?"

"Certainly Iduna. Iduna Bjorklund. Have you never heard of Bjorklund's Buggy Whips?"

"Oddly enough, never. Could we accelerate this narrative? They'll be here any minute."

"So will Iduna, that's what I am trying to tell you. Her house was blown to splinters by a tornado week before last. She has to earn a living and there's nothing for her out there, so I wrote and invited her here. She phoned today to tell me she's arriving Friday at half-past three."

Before Shandy had time to ejaculate, "My God!" the doorbell rang. He said it anyway and went to let in the guests.

Marriage was agreeing with Peter Shandy. He smiled oftener now. At fifty-six, he carried his five feet eight inches straight and springy, might have spared a few pounds but was by no means pudgy, and could still outwork any of his students in the turnip fields. He still wore his good gray suits, but his shirt and tie, chosen by Helen, were livelier in hue than they'd have been a few months ago.

All four guests arrived together, which wasn't surprising since Ames and the Enderbles were next-door neighbors. Mary Enderble looked like a lady leprechaun in a deep-green dress with a billowing skirt and snug basque. John Enderble, Professor Emeritus of Local Fauna, had brought along a baby kangaroo mouse in a matchbox lined with cotton. Having lost its mother in tragic circumstances, the infant was being weaned on an eyedropper that had to be held to its squeaking mouth every few minutes.

Helen was delighted with the mouse. Lorene McSpee didn't think mice in the dining room were very sanitary. She had on a pajama costume that exactly matched her complexion, brick red patterned in savage zigzags of brown and puce.

Professor Ames was wearing what he always wore, a tweed jacket with the elbows out and a pair of pants his son had outgrown sometime or other. Nevertheless, he looked strange. The trousers were pressed. His shirt was of a whiteness that abraded the eyeballs. His necktie didn't look as if it had been used to tie up tomato plants. Mrs. McSpee must have got the upper hand of him completely.

Shandy hastened to settle his old friend in the most comfortable chair before the housekeeper could grab it. Unmanned as he'd been by the news about Iduna Bjorklund, he began to feel that the darling of South Dakota couldn't arrive too soon. Maybe they could marry her off to Tim and get rid of Lorene. It was a shame that tornado hadn't hit sooner, so that Helen wouldn't have wasted an invitation on this ghastly woman. Not that Helen didn't feel the same way, but once she'd committed the error, she couldn't weasel out.

His new wife was good at everything except hurting other people's feelings he'd discovered and Lorene McSpee had her share of sensitivity. She was belaboring that point at every opportunity, making it clear that as a domestic worker she didn't expect first-class entertainment and that she certainly wasn't getting it here.

"Oh, I don't care. Whatever you've got the most of," was her reply when Shandy asked her what she'd like to drink. When he offered scotch, she decided she'd rather have bourbon. When she got it, she sipped and made a face. At the table she picked up her fork, examined it with a clinical eye, and observed, "I'm glad you didn't get out your sterling for me, Mrs. Shandy. I don't suppose you'd go to the bother except for somebody special."

"I'd be delighted to bother if we had any," Helen replied with a rather forced smile. "The only silver we own is a trophy Peter won in a plowing contest when he was twelve."

Fortunately, the kangaroo mouse began emitting such pitiful squeaks about half an hour after they'd left the table that John Enderble decided he'd better take it home to bed. That broke up the party, and none too soon. There was no doubt about it, Lorene McSpee had to go. Shandy made the formal declaration as he was taking off his shirt.

"Drat it, Helen, this situation is serious. That harpy has designs on Tim. Did you see her trying to cut his meat for him? What if he should turn off his hearing aid and say yes at the wrong time? That's how Jemima landed him."

"Was Jemima as awful as Lorene?"

"Nothing like. She was pushy, insensitive, opinionated, a busybody and a nonstop talker, but she wasn't vicious for the fun of it like that she-wolverine who's trying to get her hooks into him now."

"She is, isn't she? Wasn't she dreadful about the silver? I only hope to goodness Miss Flackley doesn't get the same notion, though she'd be far too well bred to say so. I'll have to drop a gentle remark that stainless is all we have."

"What are you talking about? Who's Miss Flackley?"

"Peter, you know perfectly well who Miss Flackley is. You've known her a great deal longer than I have."

"Helen, you don't by any chance mean Flackley the Farrier?"

"Of course I do. I've invited her to dinner Friday night."

"What in Sam Hill for?"

"Because she's a likable, interesting woman with an original turn of mind and I want to know her better. I asked Professor Stott, too. I think he may have his eye on her. He invited her to look at his pig."

"That would seem to indicate stirrings of the tender passion."

"Do you really think so?" asked Helen demurely. "He asked me, too, but I didn't go. After all, I'm a married woman now."

"And see that you remember it," her husband replied. "Cavorting around pigpens with that lardy Lothario ill beseems your connubial status."

"Is he really a Lothario? Whatever happened to Mrs. Stott, or wasn't there one?"

"Indeed there was, some two hundred and eighty pounds of her at last recorded estimate. So far as I know, Stott remained faithful to his Elizabeth during her lifetime, which was untimely cut short by a surfeit of herring at one of Sieglinde Svenson's little tea parties. I was one of the ten pallbearers. I was a solid mass of muscle in those days."

"Do tell. Did she leave any children?"

"Eight. Stott, as you might expect, sired two litters of quadruplets."

"What happened to them?"

"Grown and scattered. They're all successful pig farmers, sausage-stuffers, ham-curers, and whatnot. I suppose it's a lonely life for Stott without his family around, now that I think of it. Man cannot live by swine alone."

"Then I'm glad I invited him. He ought to enjoy Iduna, she's crazy about animals. I'll bet she offers to take over the night feedings for John's mouse. Oh, that's an idea! I'll ask Mary Enderble to lend me some table silver for Friday's dinner. She'll understand about Miss Flackley."

"That's more than I do," said her husband testily. "Why do you have to go bumming forks and spoons from the neighbors? Can't we buy some of our own?"

"Peter, sterling flatware costs the earth these days."

"How much earth?"

"Probably somewhere around two hundred dollars a place setting, more or less, depending on what kind you choose."

"A bagatelle. Drat it, woman, can't you get it through your parsimonious little noggin that when I thee with all my worldly goods endowed I wasn't talking chicken feed? If you want to blow two hundred of my hard-won dollars to impress the blacksmith, go ahead and blow."

"But it wouldn't be just two hundred dollars, Peter. We'd also need a setting for you and one for me and one for Iduna and one for Professor Stott."

"Two for Stott. You know how he eats. I tell you what, I have only one early class on Friday. You take that day off from the library. Porble won't mind. As soon as I'm free, we'll take a ride out to that place where you and Sieglinde bought the doodad you gave Hannah Cadwall at her going-away party."

"Oh, Peter, that was the Carlovingian Crafters. They make all their silver by hand. It's the most expensive there is. Also the loveliest," Helen added wistfully. "Are you sure you want to?"

"I think it's a sterling idea," Shandy replied. "Let's lie down and talk it over."

Chapter 2

Helen rolled down the car window a crack and settled back to gloat over the brochure she'd been secretly cherishing from her previous visit to the Carlovingian Crafters.

"Peter Shandy, you are an angel of Heaven to be doing this for me."

"Not yet I'm not," he demurred, "though I may become one any second now if that clown who's hurtling toward us doesn't get back on his own side of the road."

They were off to buy the silver, both in high humor, although Helen's was perhaps a shade higher than Peter's, he being concerned for the paintwork on his new car. Used to purchasing tractors and combines, he still hadn't adjusted to the fact that so puny a vehicle could cost so much.

He hadn't minded the expense, however, nor was there any reason why he should. As a full professor, he got a generous stipend from the college. As co-propagator with Timothy Ames of the Balaclava Buster rutabaga and more recent horticultural triumphs like Portulaca Purple Passion, he hovered on the brink of being rich.

Until he met Helen Marsh, Shandy had regarded his money somewhat as he did his back teeth, nicer to have than to be without, useful when needed, requiring a certain amount of routine care but no particular thought. Now he was finding it a positive joy, because with it he could buy things to please Helen. Swapping a few thousand dollars for the pleasure of being called an angel of Heaven was, he felt, an excellent bargain.

"Let's run through the drill again," he said. "We proceed due west to the Carlovingian Crafters, select a table service of sufficient splendor to convince Miss Flackley that she's not being treated like a peasant, blow whatever may be left of our substance on lunch at that place where you and Sieglinde had those lovely pecan muffins, then make our way south by a half east to the airport. At three-thirty on the dot, God and the airlines willing, we collect Iduna Bjorklund. Thence we race like hell back to Balaclava Junction so you can get your tiara pinned to your pompadour in time to greet our distinguished assemblage."

"Peter, I will not have you making fun of our guests."

"Who's making fun? Stott is a distinguished assemblage in and of himself."

"He may have wasted away to a shadow by now. I hope he's recovered from his shock. I meant to tell you, I went over to the animal husbandry buildings again yesterday."

"Aha! So you snuck off to the pigpens after all. Frailty, thy name is woman. Belinda having a touch of colic again?"

"No, she's fine. That wasn't what Professor Stott was upset about. It seems some bright spirit had taken all the horseshoes off the horse stalls and switched them around so they pointed down instead of up."

"Good Gad!" cried Shandy. "Now the luck will run out and Balaclava will lose the Competition."

"Professor Stott's words exactly. He sees the incident as an evil machination of the Lolloping Lumberjacks of Lumpkin Corners."

"He could be right. Or the Headless Horsemen of Hoddersville. Blood runs hot at Competition time."

"It couldn't have been some of our own students acting silly, I don't suppose?" Helen suggested mildly.

"Never! They're loyal to the core, every man Jack and woman Jill of them. You don't realize what the Annual Competition of the Balaclava County Draft Horse Association means around these parts, Helen. It's no run-of-the-mill log-pulling contest, it's more like an equine Olympics. We get teams in from all over New England, and it goes on for days. Wait till you see that Grand Opening procession with our Balaclava Blacks right up in front of the whole shebang, pulling the big wagon with the Boosters' Band playing! And all the other wagons coming along behind decked out in bunting, with those gorgeous Clydesdales and Percherons and Belgians and Suffolks groomed till you could see your face in their hides, with their brasses polished like gold and their drivers slicked up in brand-new flannel shirts. There'll be two-, four-, six-, and eight-horse competitions where you're graded on handling and condition and whatnot, and plowing contests for all levels, and bareback racing and stunt riding and horseshoe pitching and—"

"Beer guzzling," said Helen. "Yes, dear. Dr. Porble was showing me the scrapbooks over at the library. He takes better care of those old clippings and photographs than he ever did of the Buggins Collection, I must say."

Since she herself was special assistant for the Buggins Collection, Mrs. Shandy was not without prejudice on this point. However, she was too happy to stay critical.

"Speaking of plowing, I watched Thorkjeld Svenson practicing with Odin and Thor the other day. It was fantastic, that behemoth of a man and those two immense beasts, all moving as one magnificent unit."

"He'll take the Seniors' cup," said Shandy complacently. "He always does."

"Cross your fingers when you say that," Helen reminded him. "Remember those upside-down horseshoes."

"Um. I wish that hadn't happened. Not that I'm superstitious or anything, but—was that the place?"

The hand-carved sign was so discreet that Shandy had gone past it. He backed the car up, swung into a parking lot concealed behind a screen of close-planted hemlocks, and followed Helen into the long, low, brown-shingled building.

The showroom they entered was worth coming to see. The Carlovingians were artisans in the tradition of Paul Revere and Edward Winslow, working in both silver and gold. Shandy, who had resigned himself to being bored for his wife's sake, wandered from one exhibit to another, intrigued by the superb workmanship and counting the pieces, as was his wont.

He was a trifle unnerved by the prices, though he realized they were justified when he found out what the costs of precious metals had risen to. Helen and Peter admired, compared, debated, and finally settled on the handsome old fiddleback pattern ornamented by a delicate leaf design that Shandy thought rather suggested the foliage of *Brassica rapa,* or common turnip.

Once they'd made their selection, they naïvely expected the silverware would simply be wrapped up and handed over to them, but that wasn't how things were done at the Carlovingian Crafters. The pieces must be taken back to the polishing room, given a final buffing, and packed into little flannel mittens impregnated with some mysterious attar alleged to retard tarnishing. The process would take half an hour or so. In the meantime, the gracious lady who'd been assisting them suggested they might care to join a guided tour of the workrooms.

"Guided tours!" Helen exclaimed. "Do you have them often?"

"Oh yes, all the time. Mr. Peaslee should be ready to start any minute now."

Mr. Peaslee, a middle-aged man got up in what was presumably the costume of an eighteenth-century silversmith, was doing an admirable job of herding together thirty-one children from a sixth grade somewhere, one harassed teacher, three mothers who'd come along to help, and two men who were hovering along the fringes, no doubt wondering how they'd got into this. Altogether, Mr. Peaslee had quite a crowd.

However, the guide had his technique well in hand. He was brisk, informative, and expert at keeping the guests from pestering the artisans. All were sorry when the tour was over. As if to prolong the experience, the Shandys tagged along when Mr. Peaslee ushered the school group out of the building to their waiting bus. There was a good deal of tooting, waving, and screaming, then the Shandys were alone in the parking lot with Mr. Peaslee and, to their surprise, the two men who they'd thought belonged with the children.

"Now," said one of the two, neither of whom had spoken a word until now, "I wonder if we could see that strong room where all the raw gold and silver are kept?"

Mr. Peaslee smiled apologetically. "I'm afraid security regulations don't allow us to include the strong room in our tour."

"Couldn't you make an exception? My friend here and I are very much interested in the gold and silver."

"Sorry, we—"

The guide stopped short, realizing that he was staring

straight into the muzzle of a very large revolver. Helen saw it, too, and uttered a high-pitched yelp that was cut short by a hand across her mouth.

"Don't scream, lady," said the second man. "I also have a gun, and it's pointed at the back of your head. Ask your husband if you don't believe me."

"Believe him, Helen," Shandy choked.

"Okay," said the gunman. "Now, if everybody behaves nice and quiet, nothing's going to happen. If anybody tries to get smart, this lady will be shot, and that will be very bad for your corporate image, Mr. Peaslee. I think you'd better show us that strong room."

"Couldn't you take me hostage instead of my wife?" Shandy forced himself to speak quietly and make no move, although he ached to lunge at the man's throat and tear it apart.

The gunman shook his head without letting the revolver waver. "Sorry, sir, I just happen to prefer women. You walk along in front of us very, very quietly and everything will be fine."

"I don't know what Mr. Birkenhead's going to say," wailed the guide.

"We'll be out of here before Mr. Birkenhead knows what's happening. Come on, move it!"

The robbery could not possibly have been any spur-of-the moment operation. The two men knew the strong room was in a separate little building at the far end of the complex, that it was well screened by that ubiquitous shrubbery, that it was protected by an elaborate electronic warning system, and that certain things could be done to disconnect the system before it went off.

They did those things. They blew the safe with a perfectly calculated charge of explosive. They forced Shandy and the hapless Mr. Peaslee to load the gold and silver into a tan Chevy pickup van that they'd parked close to the door but well away from the factory windows. There was a great deal of precious metal, but men being prodded at gunpoint can work fast. In perhaps ten minutes, the van was full and the strong room empty.

"Thanks, gentlemen," said the man who'd done most of the talking. "Now, you two go back into the strong room and stay there for exactly fifteen minutes. After that, you can yell for the police, wet your pants, have a nervous breakdown, do anything you damn please. But for one quarter of an hour you do nothing, get it? We're taking the woman with us, and if we see a police car chasing us, or if any attempt is made to interfere with us in any way, she's dead. If we're still clean fifteen minutes from now, we'll put her out of the van safe and sound. Is it a deal?"

"It's a deal," said Helen, who appeared to be the calmest of the lot. "Try not to worry, Peter, and for goodness' sake, stay right here so I'll know where to reach you after they drop me off. Don't forget to pick up the silver. I'm afraid we're going to be awfully pressed for time."

Chapter 3

Sitting still in that rifled strong room was the hardest thing Shandy had ever done in his life. He'd known almost from the start that he loved Helen, but he had not fully realized how his entire being had become a unity with hers during the absurdly short period since they'd met at that same airport toward which they ought to be heading right now. Where in God's name had those two hoods taken her? Would they keep their word about letting her go? What if a police car happened along and they got the notion it was after them?

He forced himself not to stir, knowing that if he once began moving about, he'd be unable to prevent himself from dashing for a telephone. Mr. Peaslee, on the other hand, seemed paralyzed by shock, staring at the empty corners of the room, muttering over and over in a despairing litany, "I don't know what Mr. Birkenhead is going to say."

Shandy asked the guide once, "Won't they miss you in the factory and come looking for you?"

Peaslee only shook his head and went on brooding about what Mr. Birkenhead was going to say. At fourteen minutes and thirty-one seconds after he'd started to count, Shandy's endurance broke.

"Come on," he barked, and headed for the main showroom.

Mr. Birkenhead was there. What he said was, "Well, I daresay it was bound to happen sometime. Mrs. Pomfret, would you oblige us by phoning the police and the insurance company? Professor Shandy, I believe Mr. Williams has your parcel ready at the pickup counter."

Numbly, Shandy collected their silver and locked it in the trunk of his car wondering if Helen would ever get to use it. A couple of minutes later a police cruiser whirled up with its siren whooping and he had to explain how he had helped two gunmen steal a roomful of bullion.

A description of Mrs. Shandy, the two men who had taken her hostage, and the van they'd gone off in was broadcast over the police radio. Mr. Birkenhead had somebody bring the professor a cup of coffee, which he drank gratefully, and a plate of homemade cookies Mrs. Birkenhead had sent in for the staff. They looked delicious, but he couldn't touch them. He sat on a chair somebody had pushed under him, fists clenched, eyes on the telephone.

He didn't want to be here, he wanted to be out tearing up roads, beating the woods, howling out Helen's name, doing anything but this dreadful sitting. Still, he didn't dare budge. This was where she'd expect to find him and here he must remain. The whole police force was out searching now; surely they'd pick her up any minute.

Why were they taking so long? What if they never found her? What if she'd been—he blocked out the idea. She had to come back to him because life without her would be unthinkable. But what if she didn't?

Shandy was well on the way toward suicide when a cruiser drove into the lot and Helen rushed toward him.

"Oh, Peter!"

She was in his arms. One of them was sobbing, the other laughing, or maybe both were doing both. After a while they got themselves sorted out and Helen was able to tell her story.

"I don't know where they took me. They blindfolded me and tied me up when they got me into the van, and soon transferred me to another car. We drove around for a while; then they put me out, and I got myself untied. I was in a little dirt lane in the woods. I followed it down to a road. Finally I found a house. The woman wouldn't let me in, but she did call the police for me, and I just sat on her front steps till they came. She must have thought I was either drunk or crazy."

"Are you hurt?" Shandy asked anxiously. "Did they rough you up?"

"No, not at all. The knots weren't terribly tight. I think the tying up was simply to gain time, so I wouldn't get the blindfold off too soon and see who was driving that second car."

"Then it wasn't one of the two men we saw?"

"I don't know, but I think not. I suppose the idea was to take me in one direction while the van went off in another, so I wouldn't be able to put the police on its trail. It can't possibly get far, though. There are roadblocks everywhere. It really was a stupid sort of crime. We can identify those men who held us up, and now they're stuck with that big van full of bulky metal. They're sure to be caught, and I for one shall take delight in testifying against them. Peter, do you see what time it is? Iduna's plane will be landing before we even get there!"

As graciously as though she were leaving a tea party, Helen said good-bye to Mr. Birkenhead and his artisans, thanked the police officers who had brought her back, and hustled her still dithering husband out to their car.

They didn't talk much on the way to the airport. Helen, now that her ordeal was over, had a sudden reaction of exhaustion. She put her head back against the seat and closed her eyes. Shandy, driving faster than he generally cared to and in none too good shape emotionally himself, had to give his full concentration to what he was doing. They made it with not a minute to spare.   ,

"You go on in and meet her," said Shandy. "I'll find a place to park and join you if I can, but it looks pretty full. If you don't see me inside the terminal, come back out here to the main doors. They'll let me stop long enough to pick you up. Don't try to carry anything. You're worn out already. Let her lug her own bags or get a porter."

"Yes, darling."

Helen gave him a fast kiss and sprinted through the big glass doors. He hated letting her out of his sight, but there wasn't much else he could do. Already an airport policeman was moving toward him with a no-baloney expression. He moved on, found, as he'd expected, that parking was impossible, and had to make two tortuous circuits of the ramp before his wife appeared at the appointed spot, looking smaller and daintier than ever beside a woman in a rose-colored coat and hat, whose contours were reminiscent of the Goodyear Blimp's. Behind them was a porter, his hand truck loaded to capacity and beyond. Iduna Bjorklund had obviously come to stay.

Spent and beleaguered as he was, Shandy felt a surge of fury. How dared this human zeppelin inflict herself and all her folderols on them after the ordeal they'd been through? His lips formed a terse word. Before he could utter it, Iduna moved toward him, smiling, and he had to smile back.

It would have been impossible not to. To begin with, Iduna didn't move, she floated, buoyant and merry as a pink balloon in the hand of a child at a Fourth of July parade. Nor did she merely smile, she glowed with inner goodness that made him think of the vast iron cookstove in his grandmother's kitchen back on the farm. Here, he knew by certain instinct, was a woman who made wonderful cookies and would give you some.

How had the buggy whip heiress escaped matrimony for so many years? How could any red-blooded South Dakota bachelor sit home on a Saturday night watching Lawrence Welk when he might be camping on Iduna Bjorklund's doorstep with a box of drugstore chocolates in one hand and his heart in the other?

Perhaps she'd been holding out for Mister Right. Shandy felt a stirring of unease. Could Timothy Ames be anybody's knight in shining armor? Fond as he was of his old friend, Shandy couldn't help realizing that Iduna would be an awful lot of woman for Tim to handle. Well, no doubt they could get around that somehow. She was certainly a vast improvement over Lorene McSpee.

Vast in every sense of the word. Somehow Shandy managed to cram Iduna and her luggage into the car, got Helen perched in the only vacant corner with her feet on the one suitcase that simply would not go anywhere else, and they were off.

Rush-hour traffic was starting to build up. Back in Balaclava Junction, or wherever she lived, Miss Flackley was no doubt primping for her debut in local society. Professor Stott would be sharpening his appetite. Helen must be concerned about her dinner, but she wasn't showing it.

In fact, she was chattering away nineteen to a dozen with Iduna, catching up on everything that had happened since she left South Dakota, which seemed to be a surprising lot. The robbery, so important such a short time ago, was now relegated to a mildly amusing anecdote squeezed in between somebody's divorce and a truly remarkable incident involving two fried eggs and a slide trombone. Shandy didn't try to make head or tail of the conversation, but attended to his driving and rejoiced to hear Helen laugh again.

Though he made the best time he could, they didn't reach the Crescent until almost a quarter to six. He dropped the women off at the brick house, wrestled the luggage into the hallway, and went to put the car away down at Charlie's, a garage on Main Steet. The house he'd lived in ever since accepting his appointment to the faculty had no driveway. To make one now would mean sacrificing one of the magnificent blue spruces in the yard, which both he and Helen would rather die than do.

Anyway, it was only a few minutes' walk. Shandy hurried to get the luggage out of the hall before the guests arrived. He found it already gone and Helen and Iduna in the kitchen, still laughing and talking while they worked with the speed of light.

Ten minutes later they had the dining table set with the exquisite new silver, hors d'oeuvres laid out in the living room, and good things happening on the stove. They left Peter to put out the drinks and rushed upstairs to fix each other's hair. By the time Professor Stott came up the front steps like a slow roll of thunder, the ladies were at the door to greet him, Helen in the new lavender evening skirt she'd bought to celebrate Portulaca Purple Passion's debut, and Iduna in a confection of pink and yellow ruffles approximately six yards in circumference.

It was like playing host to the aurora borealis, Shandy thought as he brought her a Balaclava Boomerang, a local favorite compounded of home-hardened cider and homemade cherry brandy. She loved it. Iduna was ready to love everything and everybody, and it became obvious that Balaclava was going to love her.

Miss Flackley, who arrived a careful five minutes after the half-hour gowned as any faculty wife with excellent taste might be in a long-skirted shirtwaist dress of some soft brownish material with little orange flowers on it, knew all about Bjorklund Buggy Whips. It would have been hard to say which of the lady guests was more delighted with the other.

Professor Stott was clearly charmed by them both. As he purposefully masticated Helen's excellent dinner, emitting gentle grunts and whoofles of satisfaction, he kept moving his massive head slowly from side to side in happy contemplation of his fair tablemates. He beamed goodwill and bonhomie as he accepted a third helping of mashed potatoes from the rose-tipped fingers of Miss Bjorklund, the gravy boat from the utilitarian but well-groomed hand of Miss Flackley.

When he had eaten the table bare, he paid the supreme compliment of staying awake and regaling them with anecdotes of swine he had known. In contrast to the recent fiasco, this party was a triumph. Shandy was almost but not quite sorry when Professor Stott offered to escort Miss Flackley to her van, Iduna retired to the guest room, and he had Helen to himself.

"Don't you think Iduna's a darling?" said his wife as she slipped into bed.

"She's all that and then some," Shandy agreed, yawning. "Several darlings rolled into one. What do you think a runt like Tim could ever do with a woman that size?"

"Love will find out the way. Good night, dearest. Thank you for my beautiful silver."

There were a lot of things Shandy would have liked to say then, but he was too tired. Throwing an arm over Helen, he went to sleep, and so did she.

They were accustomed to early rising, but it did seem a trifle excessive when somebody came thumping on their brass knocker at half-past four the next morning. Muttering a curse, Shandy grabbed his bathrobe and rushed to get down there and slaughter whoever was making that infernal racket before Helen and their guest woke up in a panic.

He hurled open the door, amazed to confront Professor Stott, but such a Stott as he had never seen before. Stott was frantic. He grabbed Shandy by the bathrobe, shook him till he could hardly breathe, and gasped, "She's gone!"

Naturally, Shandy's first thought was of Helen. "No, no, Stott. We got her back all right. She's upstairs asleep."

"No, I'm not," said his wife behind him. "What's wrong, Professor Stott? Who's gone?"

"Belinda!" he wailed.

"Belinda? You mean your pig?"

"I mean Belinda of Balaclava," he almost sobbed. "My prize sow, the fruit of thirty years' selective breeding, the sow on whom I have pinned my hopes of the Perfect Piglet. She's gone!"

"You mean she's run away?"

"Of course she hasn't run away. Why would she run away? She had the world at her hooves. Anyway, how could she run? She weighs eight hundred fifty-three pounds and is due to farrow in three weeks. She's been kidnapped!"

"How do you know?" Shandy managed to interject.

"I received a mysterious telephone call. It aroused me from my slumbers. That would not normally be an easy thing to do."

Stott was beginning to recover some of his wonted dignity. "Perhaps I was occultly attuned to the distress which Belinda must naturally be feeling at the hands of her perfidious captors, and was sleeping less soundly than usual. In any event, I picked up the instrument and was addressed in a sinister hiss."

"A sinister hiss?"

"I cannot otherwise describe the sound. It hissed, 'Professor Stott, go look on your doormat.' That, as you will grant, was an odd sort of message to receive at an early hour of the morning. I requested elucidation but got no reply. At last it dawned on me that the connection had been broken. I cogitated for some time, then concluded that this must be some student prank.

"Since I am not insensitive to the japeries of youth, I proceeded to open the door, expecting to find there some article of a frivolous nature, and to hear snickers from the surrounding shrubberies. I heard only the soughing of wind through the boughs and the dismal hoot of some far-off owl, either *Bubo virginianus* or *Strix varia*. I am unable to state which. I am wholly overwrought. It may even have been *Strix nebulosa nebulosa*."

Stott lapsed into silent dejection, or possibly slumber. Shandy prodded him.

"What did you find on the doormat?"

"This!"

From his cavernous pocket, Stott hauled a glass jar and held it out, label foremost. The caption read, "Pickled Pigs' Feet."

"The inference, I confess, did not immediately strike

me. After further cogitation, however, I found the vague malaise which had seized me upon first hearing that sinister hiss was becoming intensified, to the point that I donned rough garments and went to reassure myself that all was well at the pigpens. To my horror, I found Belinda's gate wide open, and—" Stott collapsed into a chair and buried his face in his hands. "Forgive me. I am overcome."

"Land's sakes, who wouldn't be?"

Like a cumulus cloud on a windy summer's day, Iduna Bjorklund had wafted her bulk silently down the stairs and into the gathering. "What you need is a cup of coffee. Come with me."

She took the sufferer firmly by the hand and led him kitchenward. Shandy and his wife exchanged glances. After all, it was their house and their coffee, so they went, too. A few minutes later the four of them were seated around the kitchen table with mugs and plates in front of them. Half a dozen doughnuts did much to restore Professor Stott's wonted composure. He was able to continue his narrative.

"I searched the surrounding area, to no avail. Hampered though I was by darkness and the fact that I had forgotten to put on my spectacles, I could not have missed seeing Belinda."

"She'd have come to you," said Iduna. "A sow knows who her friends are."

"Yes," said Stott, "I believe she would. When she did not, I faced the inevitable conclusion. Belinda has been a victim of another such terrorist attack as Mrs. Shandy was so regrettably exposed to yesterday. The pigs' feet were meant as a threat."

"Oh no!"

Iduna's hand fluttered to the ruffles at the neck of her baby-blue peignoir. The garment was the size of an umbrella tent and could not have been more bewitching.

"There was only one thing to do," Stott went on, "and I did it. I went and roused President Svenson."

"At this hour?" gasped Shandy. "You're a brave man, Stott."

"Desperate situations require desperate measures. He, I regret to say, seemed inclined to treat the matter with an unbecoming levity. However, he did agree to mobilize the campus security force and institute a thorough search of the grounds. Thereupon, I deemed it wise to go back home for my eyeglasses and join the search party. As I was retracing my steps, pondering what further action might be taken without jeopardizing Belinda's position, I thought of you and the astounding percipience you displayed during the remarkable series of incidents at Illumination time."

"Oh, I shouldn't call it astounding percipience," Shandy demurred modestly.

"I should," cried Helen. "So, in short, Professor Stott, you want my husband to find out who kidnapped your pig?"

The head of animal husbandry gazed in admiration at the assistant librarian who had so swiftly divined his purpose. "That is my fervent hope. To call in the police at this juncture might be to seal Belinda's doom. Still, a man can't sit and do nothing. Surely you must understand that, Shandy!"

Shandy understood only too well. If Stott was experiencing even a tiny fraction of the agony he himself had gone through yesterday waiting to find out whether Helen would turn up alive or dead, how could any human being decline his plea? Stott, like himself, was dedicated to his research. Knowing how it felt to have a flat of tenderly nursed seedlings damp off, he could imagine how Stott must be feeling with a specimen the size of Belinda in jeopardy.

Even if this did turn out to be only the students' annual spring madness, nobody would find the joke so hilarious should the prized sow deliver her brood prematurely, then turn on the piglets and eat them, as sows had been known to do under conditions of extreme stress. What could he say except, "I'll do what I can"?

Chapter 4

Stott was wringing his hands, Helen was patting him on the shoulder, and Iduna was pouring them all another cup of coffee to keep their strength up when the telephone rang.

"I'll take it," said Shandy.

If he was to be a man of action, he might as well start now. It was probably their next door neighbor, Mirelle Feldster, wanting to know why the lights were on so early. Mirelle wasn't one to let a tidbit of news go unearthed.

No, it was not Mirelle. It was apparently somebody trying to be funny. The words came out in what might indeed have been described as a sinister hiss.

"Is Professor Stott there?"

"Yes," said Shandy testily. "Speak up, I can't hear you very well."

"Tell him to look on the doormat."

That was all. He slammed down the receiver. Helen said, "What was it, Peter?"

"Somebody wanting Stott to look on the doormat."

"Oh dear! Not more pigs' feet? Peter, I don't think this is one bit amusing."

"Neither do I."

Shandy opened the front door. A white paper parcel not more than six inches long and four inches wide was lying on the stoop. He picked it up and brought it inside.

"Looks like a package of meat."

"Then don't open it here," said Helen. "Take it out to the sink in case it drips."

"What if it's a bomb?"

"All the more reason not to mess up the new carpet."

Helen took the package out of her husband's hand and rushed it to the sink. Unhappily, she unwrapped it at the precise moment Iduna started to refill the coffeepot.

"Why, Helen," the guest remarked, "you're not planning to cook pork chops at this hour of the morning, are
you?"

"Pork chops?"

Like a bullet from a gun, or more aptly a shell from a
howitzer, Professor Stott leaped from his chair. "Where did
you get that?"

"Off the doormat," said Shandy unhappily. "Your
friend called again."

"What did he say?"

"Just asked for you and said to look on the doormat.
Don't be alarmed, Stott. That can't be one of Belinda's
chops. It's too thin."

"The paper's from the Meat-o-Mat," said Helen, referring to a store which she and many of her neighbors
often patronized. "This chop doesn't look awfully fresh to
me, and they're usually very fussy about quality. I'd say
it's been bought a while ago and kept in its original
wrapper."

"Which means it must have been obtained for the purpose to which it was put," Shandy mused. "Hence we
may infer that this was no spur-of-the-moment pignapping. I hope whoever's pulled this caper is in one of my
classes. It would give me particular pleasure to flunk him,
her, or more probably them. I'd say it was next to impossible for one person to have made off with Belinda,
wouldn't you, Stott? A gang with a flatbed truck would be
more like it. I expect we'll be able to see tire tracks as
soon as it gets light enough. The police may have picked
up a trail already."

"We must hope so."

Somewhat reassured, Professor Stott began to extricate
himself from the small kitchen. "I shall go back and lend
my personal effort to the search. Are you coming,
Shandy?"

"Not in my bathrobe. I'll meet you at the barns as soon
as I'm dressed."

Shandy turned toward the stairs, then paused. "I wonder how they knew you were coming here. You didn't
happen to notice anybody trailing you?"

"No. I was steeped in gloomy ratiocination. I would not
be difficult to follow."

That was true enough. Following Stott would be about
as hard as tracking a hippopotamus across a tennis court.

Shandy put on some warm old clothes and was back downstairs before Stott had quite decided to go on without him.
The man was still making his stately farewells to Mrs.
Shandy and Miss Bjorklund when the front door began to
buckle from thunderous blows on the knocker. This visitor
was Thorkjeld Svenson, and the President was extremely
upset.

"Shandy, you've got to find Stott."

"Nothing easier, President. Come in."

"No time. Damn it, where's Stott?"

"I am here." The professor moved into the light. "Have
you found her? Is she unharmed?"

"She's dead. Guard found her in the mash feeder."

"But that's impossible! Not—good God! Not dismembered?"

"Of course not dismembered. They just doubled her
up and shoved her in."

"President, this is an ill-timed jest. The mash feeder
is not more than two feet square. Belinda—"

"Who's talking about Belinda? It was Flackley the
Farrier. She's had her throat cut with one of her own
knives. It was in the feeder with her."

"Oh no!" cried Helen. "But she was here last evening!
We had her to dinner. We liked her so much."

"Sorry." The great man had the grace to apologize.
"Shouldn't have blurted it out like that. But, damn it, it's
a shock. Nice woman. Capable woman. Liked her myself. Sieglinde liked her. Odin and Thor liked her!"

"Even Loki liked her," said Professor Stott in a voice
of doom. "President, do you still believe my sow was kidnapped as a student prank?"

"Stott, I don't know what to think. If this was a joke
that backfired, it's the worst thing that ever struck this
college. Just tell me one thing, what the hell would Miss
Flackley be doing at the pigpens in her nightgown?"

"I cannot tell you."

"Are you sure it was a nightgown?" Helen asked him.

"Of course it was a nightgown. Thin thing with a long
skirt. What else would it be?"

"Was it brown with little orange flowers?" Helen persisted.

"How the hell should I know? What difference does it
make?"

"A great deal, I should think," said Shandy. "As my

wife mentioned, Miss Flackley dined with us last evening. She had on the sort of long dress any woman might wear for such an occasion. If Helen says it was brown with little orange flowers on it, then it assuredly was. If she was still wearing that same dress when she was killed, we can infer that she went directly from here to the pigpens."

"In her party dress?" Helen scoffed. "She wouldn't do that. Miss Flackley was a meticulous woman."

"The pigpens are scrupulously maintained," said Stott rather huffily.

"I know they are," said Helen, "but I still can't see any woman going there of her own free will late at night in such an unsuitable outfit. Unless she'd left her van up there, which seems absurd. You walked her to it, Professor Stott. Where was it?"

"In the auditorium parking lot."

'That's just down around the corner," Helen explained to Iduna. "Visitors seldom bring cars to the Crescent because parking is so awkward here. I wonder if the van's still there."

"I should be inclined to think not," said Stott. "As the hour was somewhat advanced, I waited until she had started her engine and turned on her lights before making my own departure. She was in the process of leaving the lot when I began to retrace my steps up the hill."

"Where does she live?" asked Shandy.

"I have not the remotest idea."

"Why haven't you?" roared Svenson.

"There was never any need," Stott explained with simple dignity. "We have always had a Flackley the Farrier. According to departmental tradition, Balaclava Buggins himself made an arrangement with the then Flackley the Farrier to come to the college once every two weeks and do whatever was necessary for the proper maintenance of the livestock. Flackley always came. One day the Flackley who had grown old in the service of his profession did not come. In his place was a young man, presumably his son, who did the necessary work and left without explanation. Eventually this young man became an old man and was replaced by another young man. One day this Flackley did not appear. In his stead was a woman of indeterminate years. She performed with the same capability as her predecessors. She, too, has never missed an appointment.

I assume that some other Flackley will appear a week from Tuesday and perform the usual tasks with the usual efficiency. At that point, if you so desire, I will break with tradition and obtain an address."

"The hell you will," bellowed the President. "Damn it, man, we've got a corpse in our corncrib. Somebody's got to claim the body. She must have lived somewhere. She must have relatives. According to you, there's an untapped pool of Flackley the Farriers sitting around somewhere waiting for the call to duty. How do we get in touch with them?"

"I expect the police will know how to handle that," Shandy soothed him. "Miss Flackley couldn't have lived too far from the college if she never missed an appointment even in bad weather. Come on, let's get over to the barns before they take her away. I'd like to make sure she's still dressed as we last saw her."

The three men left the Crescent and cut across the athletic field toward the college barns. Shandy, though much the smallest, outdistanced the others and got to the pigpens just as the police were lifting Miss Flackley's body out of the extremely sophisticated pig feeder which had been designed and built to Professor Stott's specifications. She made an astonishingly small bundle for a woman who'd earned her living shoeing Shire horses and Balaclava Blacks.

He thought of the farrier as he'd last seen her, smiling, a bit flushed with wine and good food, gently but firmly setting him straight on one of the lesser-known passages from the poetical works of Felicia D. Hemans. She'd been the only one at table who knew that the *D.* stood for Dorothea. It occurred to Shandy that he didn't even know what her own first name was, much less her second, and that he was more distressed by his ignorance than he could have believed possible. Damn it, he'd liked Miss Flackley as well as Odin and Loki did; why had he never taken the trouble to know her better?

To be sure, she'd never gone out of her way to encourage familiarity. She'd always kept that little screen of crisp competence around her, like a trained nurse in a private home, not wishing to be either snubbed or patronized. It must have been a lonesome life for Miss Flackley.

Or had it? For all he knew, she had a lover in every haymow. In any event, she'd had a pleasant time on her last night alive. For that, as for so many other things, he was grateful to his wife. He told the police who he was and why he was there, and they let him take a close look at the body.

"Yes, that's the dress she had on last evening," he said. "Have you any idea how long ago this—this thing happened?"

"Certainly not less than three or four hours ago, perhaps a little longer," said a man who must be a police doctor.

"Then it's quite possible she came directly here, though I can't think why she would," Shandy replied. "Our dinner party didn't break up until close to midnight."

"She didn't mention anything about checking the pig?"

"No, nor was there any earthly reason why she should have, at least not by herself. Another of our guests was Professor Stott, head of our animal husbandry department. That's he coming along the path now. Belinda—that is, the missing sow—was his particular—er—research project. If he had wished Miss Flackley's professional opinion, he would surely have come with her."

"What makes you so sure he didn't? Who saw her last when she left your house?"

"Why—er—he did. He walked her to her van, which she had left parked in the Home Arts Auditorium lot around the corner from the Crescent, where we live."

"Oh yeah?" said Fred Ottermole, Balaclava's police chief, who had managed to include himself in the interrogation. "Then what happened?"

"Then she drove off."

"And where did Stott go?"

"I suggest you ask him that question," snapped Shandy. He'd had dealings with Fred Ottermole before. It was his opinion that Fred would be well advised to go back to cruising up and down Main Street, nabbing malefactors who threw candy wrappers about in violation of Balaclava Junction's stiff anti-littering regulations.

Fred's nose was no doubt out of joint because President Svenson had been so quick to call in the highly efficient state police, thereby showing excellent sense. The last time Svenson had trusted Ottermole with a corpse, he'd wound up having two murders on his hands instead of one. He would not make the same mistake twice. Indeed, the President seldom made a mistake at all. He surely would not allow Professor Stott to be arrested for the murder of Miss Flackley just because Stott happened to have walked the farrier to her van.

Where, by the way, was that vehicle? This, at least, was something Fred Ottermole might reasonably be expected to know. Shandy asked him.

"Ottermole, where have they taken the van?"

"What van?"

"Her van, drat it! The traveling smithy with 'Flackley the Farrier' plastered all over the sides. Great balls of fire, man, you've seen it often enough. Where is it?"

"How the hell should I know?"

"Then ask, can't you? If the state police haven't driven it off, that means the murderer must have."

"Hey, yeah!" Ottermole perked up. "Say, maybe you've got something there. But why would anybody do a dumb thing like that? Cripes, it's got her name plastered all over it, like you said."

"Possibly the person was only interested in a—er—short-term loan. I'm wondering whether the purpose of attacking Miss Flackley might have been simply to get hold of the van."

"What for?"

"It's a big van. Belinda's a big pig."

Ottermole went over and spoke to the state police lieutenant in charge. A moment later they both came over to Shandy.

"What's this Ottermole's been telling me about a van, Professor?"

"Miss Flackley, the lady you just—er—fished out of that corncrib, was, as you doubtless know, a farrier," Shandy began.

"You mean she ran a boat or something?"

"No, sir. Farriers are persons who shoe horses and sometimes attend to other physical needs of farm animals, as distinguished from blacksmiths, who actually forge horseshoes and do other iron work. A farrier, of course, may be a blacksmith, but I have the impression that Miss Flackley's practice consisted exclusively of farriery."

"Are you putting me on?" the lieutenant demanded.

"No, sir, I am not. Flackleys have always been farriers."

"And why shouldn't they be?" said a nearby sergeant who happened to be of the same sex as the body she had helped to carry. "What's wrong with a woman being a farrier?"

"Nothing, nothing," Shandy assured her. "Miss Flackley was an extremely competent one, an ornament to her profession. She shared Professor Stott's concern for Belinda's welfare, and was, I believe, able to give him valuable advice on more than one occasion."

"Belinda?" said the lieutenant. "That's the pig that got stolen, right? Was it sick?"

"Not at all, so far as I know. At last report, Belinda was in the pink of condition. She is, however, in an—er—advanced state of pregnancy."

"To kidnap a sow in her state," added Professor Stott, who had finally lumbered up to the group, "was a reckless, cruel, and utterly despicable thing to do. I cannot imagine any student of Balaclava Agricultural College stooping to such infamy. I cannot imagine *anybody*—"

"Sure, we get the picture," interrupted the lieutenant. "You're Professor Stott, right? So you were the last person to see Miss Flackley alive?"

The professor cogitated. At last he shook his majestic head.

"I cannot subscribe to that assumption. The logical inference would then be that I was also the person who killed her. That, I am able to assure you, was not the case."

"How are you able to assure me? You walked her to her van, right?"

"That is correct."

"The van was parked where?"

"Beside the Home Arts Auditorium, facing Prospect Street."

"What happened then?"

"I assisted her into the cab. She started the motor, switched on the lights, and drove off."

"In what direction?"

"I cannot say. I was fatigued. The hour was advanced. Having performed what I conceived to be my duty as an escort, I did not stay to watch her out of sight, but turned and began walking back up the hill toward my own house."

"Where do you live?"

"On Valhalla."

"Come again?"

"Valhalla is a name facetiously given to the hill up behind the campus where President Svenson, myself, and a number of other faculty members have our homes."

"You didn't happen to come past these barns on the way?"

"No, I proceeded in a direct line from my starting point. That is, I passed the Shandys' house and continued on the path that stretches up across the campus to connect with the street upon which I reside. There seemed no reason to do otherwise. Had I but known what perfidy was brewing—"

"Yeah, well, that's how it is with perfidy," said the lieutenant. "Did you meet anybody on the way?"

"Possibly. I do not recall. I was lost in thought."

"What were you thinking about?"

"My thoughts were of a private nature," the professor replied with immense dignity. "I cannot imagine they would be germane to your inquiry. However, I think I can fairly state that, among other things, I was ruminating on the desirability of drinking a glass of hot milk before going to bed. I subsequently did so, should you care for that information."

"Who fixed it for you?"

Stott surveyed the officer calmly with his small, bright blue eyes.

"I heated the milk myself. Since the death of my wife, I have become accustomed to performing small domestic tasks."

"Then you live alone? You don't have a housekeeper or anybody?"

"An extremely capable woman named Mrs. Lomax comes twice a week to clean the house. I take most of my meals at the faculty dining room. I do not require a live-in servant. Am I to infer that you are giving me an opportunity to provide what I believe is known as an alibi and that I am failing to do so?"

"Oh, I wouldn't go that far," said the lieutenant. "Mind taking a look at the body? Can you tell me if this is exactly the way Miss Flackley was dressed when you last saw her?"

"No," said Professor Stott after a thoughtful scrutiny, "it is not. Having four daughters and four daughters-in-law, I have been compelled to develop an awareness of sartorial detail. Aside from the bloodstains now so lamentably present, the gown itself is the same. The ornamental objects adorning her person, an old-fashioned gold locket and bracelet, are the same. However, you doubtless observe that the material of her gown is thin and last evening was chilly. When I last saw her, she had enveloped herself in a length of heavy brown material known, I believe, as a stole. The stole was of mohair yarn. Mohair is obtained from the fleece of the angora goat. I could give you some interesting statistics about the angora goat if you wish."

"Some other time," said the lieutenant. "Sergeant Mullins, start searching the grounds for a brown mohair stole."

"While you're at it," Sandy put in, "you might keep an eye out for a large brown van that says 'Flackley the Farrier' on the sides. I expect you'll find the stole in the van."

The state policeman seemed a bit weary of hearing about the van. He looked Shandy up and down once or twice, then asked, "You a friend of this gentleman?"

"Of Professor Stott?"

Shandy was a trifle embarrassed by the question. The men of Balaclava were not accustomed to parading their feelings for one another, except in cases of open enmity. He searched for words.

"I believe I am entitled to claim that relationship. We have been colleagues for over eighteen years. I was a pallbearer at his wife's funeral. He has been a frequent guest at my house."

"He was there all last evening, right?"

"I thought we'd established that."

"And so was this Miss Flackley, right? How come you invited them together?"

"I didn't invite them at all," Shandy replied. "My wife did. Not that I wasn't pleased to have them, of course."

"Sure. So why did your wife invite them together?"

"Bcause she thought it would be a good idea, I suppose. If you're trying to intimate that she or I or anybody else thought of Professor Stott and Miss Flackley as a—er—couple, you're barking up the wrong tree. My wife has not lived at Balaclava long. She was previously unacquainted with Miss Flackley. Happening to fall into conversation with her and finding her an interesting person, she issued a spur-of-the-moment invitation to dinner.

As I understand, Professor Stott was there, so she asked him, too. Wasn't that the way of it, Stott?"

"It was. Miss Flackley seemed surprised, though pleased, by the invitation. I myself was of a similar sentiment. Mrs. Shandy is a lady of excellent heart and great skill in the culinary art. She spoke of noodle pudding. I accepted with alacrity."

"No doubt," said the state policeman doggedly, "but what were you and Miss Flackley doing together at the time?"

"Miss Flackley was trimming the off hind hoof of Odin, one of our college horses. I was making my way toward the pigpens to visit Belinda, about whom I had been experiencing a slight anxiety. Having respect for Miss Flackley's acumen in such matters, I paused to ask her to accompany me. Miss Flackley subsequently diagnosed Belinda's ailment as nothing more than a touch of colic and prescribed a slight modification in diet. Belinda has a sensitive stomach."

A spasm that was more than colic passed over Stott's nobly porcine countenance. "And while we stand here bandying trivialities, God knows what may be happening to her."

"You call murder a triviality, Professor?"

"No," replied Stott, "I call it infamous! And I call it equally infamous to be kept here answering irrelevant questions when I ought to be out hunting for my sow. Sir, I can no longer submit to this interrogation. I, too, have my duty."

The police lieutenant shrugged. "Okay, go ahead and search. Officer Partinger here will go with you. Don't try to lose him."

"Why would I do that?" asked Stott in all innocence. "We need every searcher we can muster. Shandy, are you coming? President?"

"Shandy can't come," said Svenson. "I'll be along later. Right now I'm going to call a general assembly and put the fear of God and of Me into every student on this campus. You want action, Stott. You'll get it."

Chapter 5

There wasn't an empty seat in the bleachers. All the students were decently covered, since Sieglinde Svenson was not one to stand for any nonsense about freedom of expression, but the coverings ranged anywhere from a bathrobe to a bedspread. A general assembly sprung on them at a quarter to six on a Saturday morning had left no time for titivation.

Down in front of the stands stood Thorkjeld Svenson. They'd had no time to rig a microphone, but he didn't need one. Even in the farthest reaches of the topmost seats, nobody was missing a word.

"I'm holding each and every one of you personally responsible for finding Miss Flackley's murderer and bringing back Belinda of Balaclava safe and sound," he roared. "I'm not accusing you. I can't imagine any member of this college pulling such a damn-fool stunt, but if you know anything about who did, if you saw or smelled or even thought about anything fishy going on around the pigpens last night you'd better spill it fast. This is no time for false loyalties. You know where your duty lies, and by yiminy, you're going to do it!"

He reached over and grabbed the state police lieutenant, who, although a big man, looked puny beside him. "If you have anything to say, stop on your way out and say it to Lieutenant Corbin here. If you find out anything later, come and tell me, or Professor Shandy, who's going to be acting as liaison with the police."

That was news to Shandy, but he knew better than to argue.

"Now," Svenson went on, "I'm declaring all classes and and extracurricular activities suspended until we get some results. Every one of you, get back to your dorms and put on your working clothes. Get down to the cafeteria and eat your breakfasts, then form parties and start searching. You all know Flackley the Farrier's van, and you ought to know what a pig looks like. And you've all got heads, or reasonable facsimiles. Use them. Stay out of trouble. Remember you're dealing with one or more murderers. Don't try to be heroes. Anything you find, you come back and report, fast. Dismissed!"

The stands emptied. Students surged down the field, gabbling among themselves. Looking at the sea of healthy young faces, Shandy felt a surge of pride. They were a remarkably decent lot, by and large.

None of them came forth with any information. That wasn't surprising. Nobody would dare approach Thorkjeld Svenson with a futile question or a cock-and-bull story. Nobody bent on amorous dalliance would have been apt to choose the pigpens for a late-night rendezvous. Anyway, Balaclava students worked so hard they did little after-hours roistering, except on Saturday evenings. And if any student or students had by any chance got mixed up in a mess like this, they'd hardly come waltzing up to the President in open assembly and say so.

Svenson had mentioned in his talk that the security guards had not been aware of any disturbance. That was interesting. Now that former security chief Grimble had been fired for moral turpitude and neglect of duty, those who'd escaped the ax were more righteously vigilant than ever before. On duty last night had been Silvester Lomax and his brother Clarence, both of them sharp as tacks and straight as dies. They couldn't be corrupted and they couldn't be hoodwinked, but they might possibly have been dodged by somebody who knew how their rounds were scheduled. That would be tricky because the routes were changed on alternate nights, but not impossible because each had so much ground to cover.

There'd have had to be fast footwork at the pigpens, though, Belinda's captors must have been either very well organized or very lucky. Shandy pondered the possibilities.

Pigs had something innately ridiculous about them.

One's first impulse was to look on Belinda's disappearance as a joke that had gone wrong, and one's thoughts therefore turned naturally to some of the less dedicated students. Yet Belinda was in solemn fact an extremely valuable animal. Works of art were stolen not for resale but for ransom these days; why not a pedigreed sow? If professional crooks were involved, Miss Flackley's murder didn't seem quite so incredible.

But would real criminals fiddle around making phone calls in a sinister hiss and planting oddments of delicatessen on doormats instead of down-to-business ransom notes? Why hang around and take such risks of being spotted, unless somebody had a lot of gall and a perverted sense of humor?

Somebody did. This wasn't the first sick joke that had been pulled in the past couple of nights. Shandy thought of those eight inverted horseshoes. That little caper hadn't been accomplished in a minute, or without a certain amount of noise, and the security guards hadn't caught the perpetrator then, either.

Helen had told him Stott suspected the Lumpkin Corners crowd of that one, and he himself had mentioned the Hoddersville team, only half in jest. If a bunch of the boys were whooping it up at Sam's place or somewhere handy, they just might have got to thinking it would be a jolly idea to swipe Stott's pet pig. They might also know how the security schedule was handled, because things did tend to get around in small villages like these. He couldn't imagine any horseman's cutting the farrier's throat on purpose but a burly drunk struggling with a tiny woman might well do her an injury by accident, maybe without even noticing, and stuff her into the mash feeder thinking she'd only fainted from shock or something. It was farfetched, but not impossible.

So Shandy found himself juggling four possibilities: that the sow had been taken by students meaning a practical joke, by crooks looking for ransom, by competitors trying to demoralize their archrival, or by somebody else for some other reason. A fat lot of help that was.

At least Belinda was probably still alive, though she may well have been tranquillized to keep her quiet while she was being taken away. A sow the size of Belinda would be easier to transport alive than dead, and there had been no blood around except Miss Flackley's. If Belinda's throat had been cut, too, the place would have been ankle-deep in gore. "Bleeding like a stuck pig," was no fanciful metaphor.

As to whether her safety would be enhanced by having several hundred young zealots out looking for her, he wasn't so sure. However, he could see why Svenson had turned them loose. With the weekend coming up, they'd all have cut whatever classes they had and gone anyway. Organized groups were less apt to get into serious trouble than individual searchers.

Of course if this was a student prank gone wrong, what better cover could the perpetrators have than to be out scouring the woods with their classmates? Shandy wished he could honestly believe in those professional crooks or even the bunch of drunks from Hoddersville, but in ugly truth, the simplest explanation was apt to be the correct one.

He could see all too clearly how the abduction of Mrs. Shandy that same morning might give some muttonhead the notion of staging a parody, and how Belinda might be a logical target. He could see that Miss Flackley's unaccustomed presence on campus during the evening would suggest the feasibility of using her van to transport the pig. He could envision her being flagged down after she'd left the Home Arts parking lot and asked to go up to the barns because some animal had been taken ill suddenly.

Perhaps the idea was to shut her in one of the barns while the pig was being taken off in the van, but Miss Flackley wouldn't take kindly to being manhandled. She was a great deal stronger and smarter than might have been expected. Perhaps she'd snatched up the knife to defend herself, and somehow got her own throat cut in the melee. He could see the frantic pranksters who'd so abruptly and horribly become murderers, for certainly this could have been no one-person job, doubling up her body and thrusting it into the mash feeder to get it out of sight. But how could they then have gone ahead with kidnapping Belinda and sending those ridiculous tokens to Stott?

Maybe they thought they had to, so they could pretend they'd left Miss Flackley alive and that her death had nothing to do with the joke they were trying to pull. The pigs' feet and the pork chop had, after all, been delivered before the official announcement was made, so they might have been able to make out a case for themselves. Perhaps they'd even be telling the truth. Could she have been left shivering at the pigpens with or without her mohair stole, only to have somebody else come along and scrag her?

Who, for instance? What was the sense in trying to speculate before he had any data to work from? He might as well at least go call Helen and let her know he'd been delegated to the no doubt thankless task of pestering the police for information they wouldn't want to give him. He went to the phone in the ticket office.

There was a local phone book beside it, and on impulse he spun the pages, looking for a Flackley listing. There was none. He thought about this a moment, then rang up Moira Haskins, who had taken the late Ben Cadwall's place as comptroller.

"Mrs. Haskins, sorry to bother you so early, but something has come up and I've got to get at the records right away. Could you come over and open your office?"

Mrs. Haskins, who had no doubt been awakened from well-earned sleep, was not happy at the request. "Who is this, anyway? What's happened?"

"Oh, sorry. It's Peter Shandy, and I'm afraid the news is very bad. Miss Flackley, the farrier, has been murdered."

"You're kidding!"

"It's not a subject on which I'd be likely to jest. She was found an hour or so ago, doubled up in Belinda of Balaclava's feeding box."

"You mean the pigpen? For God's sake, why?"

"Apparently it has something to do with the fact that the pig has been kidnapped."

The comptroller emitted a snort of laughter, than caught herself.

"This is crazy! None of the kids would steal Belinda. They're all making book on how many babies she's going to have. I'm betting on seven, myself."

Shandy couldn't help thinking what a refreshing change Moira Haskins was from Ben Cadwall, though she obviously didn't know much about pigs.

"You haven't a prayer," he told her. "Seventeen would be more like it."

"Yeah?" Mrs. Haskins sounded as if she were yawning, as no doubt she was. "Sounds like a plot by P. G. Wodehouse."

"Wodehouse was funny. This is not. Mrs. Haskins, the state police have just carted Miss Flackley's body off in a large plastic bag. Her van has disappeared. Nobody knows where she lived or how to reach her people, if she has any. Since you paid her bills, you must have her address."

"Oh. Sorry, Professor. I'll meet you there in about ten minutes."

Shandy went back and explained his plan to Lieutenant Corbin, got a grunt of approval and an injunction to hurry back with the information, and walked up the long path to the administration building. He didn't really expect Mrs. Haskins to be there in ten minutes and she wasn't, but she arrived soon after, driven by her husband, who was unshaven, wearing a duffel coat over his pajamas, and agog for details of the murder. Shandy told them what little he knew, then left Haskins sitting in the car while he and Moira went into the aged brick building that had once been almost all there was to Balaclava Agricultural College.

Sure enough, the files produced a sheaf of invoices, penned in a schoolteacherish hand on yellowed but elegant billheads the original Flackley the Farrier must have had printed back when they did such things with grace and panache. The address was simply, "Forgery Point."

Shandy dimly remembered going there once with some of his colleagues on a fishing trip. The picture he retained was of mile after mile of grown-over slash, a few shabby clapboard houses, and a disproportionate number of wrecked automobiles. It seemed an odd sort of place for the impeccable Miss Flackley to spring from, though it did occur to him that "Forgery Point" might be related not to crime but to blacksmithing. Perhaps the Flackleys' forge had been the original reason for the settlement. He wondered if the smithy still existed, and if Miss Flackley had ever used it herself.

The Haskinses gave Shandy a lift back to the animal husbandry area hoping, he suspected, to get a sight of the action. However, there wasn't much to see except a couple of police cars and a few people milling around, not appearing to be doing anything in particular, although they probably were. He thanked the comptroller and her husband, mentioned that a giant pig hunt was in progress should they care to participate, and took his information back to Lieutenant Corbin as ordered.

"Forgery Point?"

The officer scratched his head. "That's a new one on me. Where the heck is it, do you know?"

"Vaguely. It's somewhere beyond the Seven Forks. I can't recall offhand which fork one takes, but I think I'd know once I got that far."

"Come on, then."

They got into one of the waiting cruisers and started twisting their way over the narrow back roads. Though the distance was not great, it took them over twenty minutes to get to Seven Forks as the snake crawls, and another twenty to navigate the ruts and potholes as far as Forgery Point.

The place was as desolate as Shandy had remembered it, but it did have a general store of sorts. Rightly surmising that this must also be the post office, the two men went in and asked the blowsy woman in charge where Flackley the Farrier lived. She eyed them with avid curiosity.

"What are you arrestin' her for?"

"Nothing," said the lieutenant with admirable restraint. "We just want to talk with some member of her family."

"She ain't got none."

"We understood the Flackleys were a large family," said Shandy in his most sternly professorial tone.

"They're all gone."

"Then we'd like to see where she lives. Could you tell us, please?"

After a good deal of fishing to find out what they were there for, the woman gave up and grudgingly imparted directions in as confusing a manner as possible. Since there was really only one road, however, they managed to locate what must be Miss Flackey's home.

The place looked as immaculate as the woman herself had been. Though the house must be edging toward the two-hundred mark, its weathered shingles were all in place, its ridgepole straight as an arrow, its chimney bricks well pointed. There were neat little brick-edged plots that no doubt would have been planted with Patient Lucy and other old-fashioned annuals if Miss Flackley had lived till the ground warmed up.

"It's a damned shame," said Corbin.

Shandy nodded. "Yes, she was a good woman. Do I see someone—"

The door opened. A man's voice called out, "That you, Aunt Martha?"

So the farrier had not been alone in the world, after all. The man who appeared in the doorway looked exactly like the sort of nephew one would expect Miss Flackley to have, not large in the frame but well muscled and wiry. His hair was dark, wavy, and plentiful, his eyebrows thick, his mustache enormous and dashingly twisted at the ends, his beard short but bushy. What little they could see of his face wasn't bad-looking. Probably in his late thirties, Shandy thought. He had on clean brown corduroys and a clean plaid flannel shirt such as his aunt herself might have worn. Shandy didn't recall her having mentioned a nephew at dinner, but neither had she alluded to any other details of her personal life.

The man didn't seem at all disconcerted to see two strangers in a police cruiser. He merely remarked, "Oh, sorry, I was expecting my aunt back. If you're looking for her, I'm afraid she ain't around right now. She went to visit some friends last night and she never came in. I guess she must of slept over. Anything I can do for you?"

"You're her nephew, eh?" said the lieutenant. "Live here right along?"

"No, I've only been here a couple of days. I was passing through the area and thought I'd stop and see what the old homestead looked like. My grandfather used to talk about Forgery Point a lot. I think he'd of been as well pleased to stay on, but it never came to be his turn."

"His turn for what?"

"Well, see, the way it's always been, when anything happens to Flackley the Farrier, whoever's handiest steps in and takes over. If there's more than one son, for instance, the oldest one gets the job and the rest light out for themselves. That's what my grandfather did. Aunt Martha's father was Flackley the Farrier for quite a while, then he took sick and died all of a sudden during World War II while the rest of'em was off in the army, so Aunt Martha quit schoolteaching and took over."

"Who taught her the craft?" asked Shandy.

"Shucks, no Flackley ever has to be taught how to shoe a horse or ram a pill down one's throat, for that matter. It's born in the blood. You might think farriery was kind of heavy work for a woman her size, but it don't seem to faze her none."

"Why didn't one of the men take over from her when they came back from the war?"

"Wasn't many came back," said the nephew. "Anyway, once you start you mostly keep on. That's the way it's always been. Say, I don't mean to be nosy, but who are you folks? I hope there ain't anything the matter."

"I'm afraid there is," said the lieutenant. "What's your name, by the way?"

"Flackley," the man replied in some surprise. "Frank Flackley. What's wrong? She been in an accident or something? Is she hurt bad?"

"I'm sorry to tell you that she's dead."

"Dead?"

Frank Flackley looked at them for what seemed like a long time. Then he drew a long breath.

"Looks like it's up to me, then. Is the van busted up much?"

"It wasn't an automobile accident, Mr. Flackley. Your aunt was the victim of a murderous assault, and the van appears to have been stolen."

"Oh, my God! Who done it?"

"We have no idea, I'm sorry to say."

Corbin filled in what few details he could give. Flackley kept shaking his head in obvious dismay.

"Now what the hell am I supposed to do? Aunt Martha told me we've never disappointed a customer, not once in a hundred and eighty-two years. I hate like hell to let the family down at a time like this, but I don't know where I'm s'posed to be at. The schedule's in the van."

He appeared more disturbed about the business than about his aunt. Perhaps to a Flackley, that was a natural reaction.

"Brace up," said Shandy. "The entire student body of Balaclava Agricultural College is out combing the hillsides right now. They may already have spotted your van. Mind if we use the telephone to check back with the college?"

"Isn't one. Aunt Martha said they never brought the lines out here."

"Good heavens! That's rather unusual, isn't it? You really are isolated, aren't you?"

"Looks like I'm gonna be," said Flackley with a grim attempt at a smile. "Don't know but what I might see about having one run in, myself. I'm used to having things a little livelier than this."

"But didn't your aunt have any friends she'd want to call up? What about business appointments?"

"Friends, I dunno. Business she woudn't need a telephone for. The work was planned out on a regular schedule, see, and the schedule was posted up in the van in case some other Flackley had to take over without notice, like now." He shook his head as if denying the fact.

"You said you were just passing through," said Lieutenant Corbin. "Mind telling us where you came from?"

"Everywheres, just about. I was travelin' with a rodeo, see, out through Wyoming, Montana, Idaho, Colorado, Nevada, you name it. Wasn't a big outfit. You never heard of Rudy's Rough Riders, I don't suppose?"

"You were a cowboy?"

"No." Again that incredulous stare. "I was the farrier, naturally. Shod the horses, doctored the animals when they got hurt, doctored the riders, too, more often than not. Ol' Doc Flackley, they used to call me, that and a few other things. Anyway, Rudy managed to hook himself a rich rancher's widow down a ways out from Santa Fe, so he busted up the outfit. Well, that left me without a job, but I had a few bucks in my pocket and I'd always sort of had a hankering to see where my folks come from, so here I am. Sort of like what they'd call the workings of fate, ain't it?"

Shandy thought of something else it might be called. An out-of-work rodeo hand could conceivably not be all that averse to taking over a prosperous family business. He could tell the same notion was running through Corbin's mind when the lieutenant asked, "Where's your car, Flackley?"

"Never needed none, traveling with the rodeo. I was aiming to get me some wheels when I got settled somewheres."

"How did you get here?"

"Wrote Aunt Martha I was headin' this way and what bus I'd be on. I figured if she wanted to meet me, she could. If not, I'd just keep ridin'. When I got to the big shopping center down there a ways, I seen the van with Flackley the Farrier on it hauled up right smack beside the bus stop, so I got off. Aunt Martha seemed real pleased to see me. Guess it's been kind of lonesome for her since the old man died. She wanted me to stay on awhile, so I said I would."

"When did this happen?"

"Day before yesterday, about three o'clock, I guess."

"Yet she went out to dinner last night, leaving her long-lost nephew here alone," said Shandy.

"I told her to go ahead, I didn't mind. After spendin' most of the week on a Greyhound bus, I was just as well pleased to stretch out in front of the TV with a couple o' beers."

"Then she did have electricity in the house."

"Sure. She run her own dynamo out back. Guess I'd better poke around and see if I can figure out how it works."

"Mr. Flackley," Shandy persisted, "aren't you rather taking things for granted? What makes you so sure you'll be the one to inherit the—er—aegis of office?"

"Well, for one thing, I'm here," said the farrier. "For another, I don't know's there's anybody else left. According to what Aunt Martha said, the Flackleys have sort of petered out. I can't say I'm exactly kickin' up my heels at the idea of spendin' the rest of my life out here with the chipmunks, but at a time like this it just don't seem decent to leave."

"You couldn't be more right about that, Mr. Flackley," Lieutenant Corbin assured him. "You'd be extremely unwise to try to leave the area before we've found out who murdered your aunt. We'll get back to you as soon as we have any news."

"Say, can't I come along with you folks and help hunt for the van? That way I might get on with my work a little faster."

"I wouldn't count on being able to use your van for a while after it's found, Mr. Flackley," said Corbin. "We may have to hold it for evidence."

"What kind of evidence? Aunt Martha wasn't killed in it, was she?"

"We don't know. Her body was found stuffed into a feeding apparatus in a barn where one of the college pigs was kept. Whether she was killed there or elsewhere hasn't yet been determined. To further complicate the situation, the pig is missing, too, and we're theorizing that the van was stolen to take the pig away."

"What the hell for?"

"Belinda of Balaclava is a very valuable animal," said Shandy.

"Yes, but, jeez! Using the family van to steal a pig. That—that's awful! You think maybe Aunt Martha was trying to stop whoever stole the pig and that's how she got killed?"

"That's as reasonable a supposition as any," said Corbin.

"But who the hell would murder a nice woman like Aunt Martha for a mess of pork chops?"

"I doubt if the pig was taken to be butchered," Shandy explained. "She may possibly have been kidnapped in the hope of extorting a ransom from the college. There have already been—er—threatening messages. You see, Belinda is no ordinary sow. She is a vital link in a chain of genetic experiments which Professor Stott of our animal husbandry department has been conducting over a period of almost thirty years and is almost due to farrow. The piglets she produces, it is hoped, will constitute a major step forward in pig breeding. Therefore, while her value in money alone is not inconsiderable, her importance to the science of swine breeding may be almost incalculable."

"Oh, now it begins to make sense. Was Aunt Martha taking care of the pig?"

"She was one of a—er—team of consultants. Professor Stott valued your aunt's opinions highly. She will be a great loss to the college. And—er—to you, too, I'm sure."

"Well, see, I hardly knew her," the nephew confessed. "It wouldn't be right for me to carry on as if I'd lost my best buddy, would it? But, well, we seemed to be getting along pretty good. The more I think about her, the worse I feel, if you really want to know. I was sort of counting on—oh, you know—maybe spending Thanksgiving and Christmas with her, havin' a place that was kind of like home. It's sure not going to be any picnic, staying here by myself."

Corbin looked around him at the forest pressing in on the neat old house. "Must be lonesome as hell out here in the wintertime. I wonder how she stood it."

"I asked her that myself," said Flackley. "She said she never minded being alone, she could always find something to do. Lot of work to an old place like this. I'll sure never be able to keep it up the way she did, unless I can find me a wife. Don't know any pretty ladies that like to cook and clean house and wouldn't mind settlin' down with a lonesome blacksmith, by any chance?"

"You never can tell," said Shandy. The buggy whip heiress flashed into his mind. Flackley impressed him as a decent sort. But that would still leave Tim with Lorene McSpee. If it was cleaning Flackley wanted, perhaps he'd do better with the demon housekeeper. It would be awful to have that woman slopping bleach water over Miss Flackley's domain, though. Shandy, like the nephew, was feeling a deepening sense of loss. It was a damned shame that so useful a life could so wantonly have been snuffed out, that so self-respecting a human being could have been handled at the end with so little regard for the dignity she'd always maintained.

Corbin had made a good point there, about not knowing whether or not she'd been killed in the place where she was found. Being at her home, seeing how meticulously she'd kept everything up, he found it less and less possible to believe she'd driven the van up to the animal husbandry area of her own free will. To visit the barns at a totally unaccustomed hour, wearing an evening dress and a mohair stole, would have been totally out of character for her. Ergo, she probably didn't.

Unless Stott was lying. Miss Flackley had, after all, been a woman, and a surprisingly charming one when she'd shed her working clothes and professional manner. Stott was by no means an unattractive man. Helen and Iduna had both gone on at some length about that very subject last night when they were straightening up after the party.

Stott was distinguished in his field, stately in presence, well lined in pocket. He had shown himself to the lonely farrier as a man susceptible to her femininity as well as respectful of her professional acumen. If by any remote chance he had asked Miss Flackley to hie with him to the pigpens to contemplate Belinda by moonlight, would she have said him nay? Wouldn't she, figuratively speaking, have thrown her mohair stole over the windmill and gone?

Stott had said he'd left Miss Flackley at the parking lot and walked home alone, but had he? Was it remotely possible the man could have deceived them all? Shandy thought back to the dinner party. Stott had been the success of the evening, no question about that, stuffing himself with Helen's good food, basking in the admiration of the other ladies, acting almost frolicsome, for him. He'd never appeared more open, more genial, more likable. Shandy found it simply incredible that Stott could have been plotting the whole time to murder Miss Flackley, stuff her into the mash feeder, and kidnap his own sow with the farrier's van. Yet when other possibilities were eliminated, the insane became the probable.

The hell with that. Other possibilities had not been eliminated. There must be scads of them kicking around. It was only a matter of finding out what they were. Corbin seemed an intelligent man; he wouldn't be taken in by the falsely obvious. Would he?

Chapter 6

Shandy had not overestimated the state policeman's intelligence. As Lieutenant Corbin seemed on the point of departing, he paused and remarked ever so casually, "Mind if we take a quick look around the house, Flackley? I didn't bring a search warrant with me, so you can refuse if you want."

The former rodeo hand shrugged. "Guess that wouldn't keep you out for long, would it? Sure, walk right in and make yourselves to home."

"Just a second. I might as well see if there's any word on the van."

Corbin went back to his cruiser and picked up the radio transmitter. "Have Madigan bring a radio car to the Flackley house at Forgery Point."

He gave marvelously accurate instructions. "No, nothing yet. . . . Nothing on the van either, eh? . . . We've got a nephew of the deceased here. Mr. Flackley has no access to a phone and is anxious to be kept informed."

He broke off the connection. "Okay, Flackley, you're in business. Soon as anything turns up, we'll send the news along by radio. In the meantime, you'll have Officer Madigan for company."

"Say, that's real nice of you," said Flackley, "but wouldn't it be just as well if I rode back with you and went out with the search parties? Don't seem right, everybody else out doin' all the work and me sitting here twiddling my thumbs."

"Try not to think of it that way, Mr. Flackley. Somebody's got to keep the home fires burning you know. How are you fixed for food, by the way? Want Officer Madigan to pick anything up along the road?"

"No, I'm fine for now, thanks. Aunt Martha stocked up as soon as she found out I was coming."

She'd done that, Shandy thought, and then some. The old-fashioned pantry shelves revealed a strange hodgepodge: cans of chili and frijoles next to Boston baked beans, bags of potato chips and pretzels rubbing labels with Quaker Oats and homemade preserves. The refrigerator—Lieutenant Corbin wasn't bashful about making a thorough search, warrant or no warrant—held the usual things like eggs and milk and cheese along with plastic-wrapped spareribs, barbecued chickens, and four six-packs of beer, one of them half empty. Miss Flackley had evidently made a touching effort to lay in the sorts of foods she thought her nephew might prefer.

This visit of his must have been a real milestone in her isolated life. Why in Sam Hill hadn't she mentioned that she was going to have the fellow staying with her? Helen would have told her to bring him along, then she'd have had a bodyguard and this tragedy might never have occurred. Shandy voiced the thought.

"Aunt Martha would never do a thing like that," Flackley replied. "She wouldn't have wanted a roughneck like me trailing along when she went out in society."

"We're not society."

"You would be to her, college professors and all. Being an educated woman herself, she could hold up her end okay, but shucks, I wouldn't even know which fork to use."

The word "fork" gave Shandy a small jolt. Just about this same time yesterday, he'd been sweating it out at the Carlovingian Crafters. Those identical forks with which Miss Flackley ate her last meal on this earth had been locked in the trunk of his car.

"Speaking of forks," he said to Corbin, "I hope to God you've caught those two rats who held up the Carlovingian Crafters yesterday."

The police officer looked at him curiously. "You own stock in the company or something?"

"No, but I helped carry out the loot. It was my wife they took hostage."

"For Pete's sake! Sure, Professor Shandy from Balaclava College. Funny I didn't make the connection. This other business put the robbery clean out of my mind. You folks have been having quite a time of it, haven't you?"

"You might say that," Shandy replied grimly. "The most bizarre part of the whole story is that we were buying the silver partly because Miss Flackley was coming to dinner. My wife"—he chose his words carefully, in order not to offend the nephew—"wanted to set an attractive table."

"Any special reason?"

"Because it was the first time we'd invited her, I suppose. Frankly, I sometimes find my wife's motives a trifle obscure."

Corbin grinned. "I know the feeling. Well, Professor, I wish I could tell you we've got those crooks safe in the slammer, but I can't. We were sure we'd be able to scoop them right in with the good descriptions we had and the weight of the stuff they were trying to get away with, but they seem to have dropped clean out of sight."

"Say," Flackley broke in, "I saw that story about the robbery on the news last night. You don't suppose by any chance they killed Aunt Martha so's they could steal our van to haul away the gold and silver."

"Taking along a thousand-pound pig in case they happened to want a ham sandwich on the way?" said Corbin mildly.

The nephew flushed. "Okay, I guess it was a dumb idea. The guys must be over the border by now, anyway. That's how they'd do it out west, have a plane or a helicopter waiting, transfer the loot while they was holding the hostage, and be halfway to Mexico by the time you started thinking about setting up a roadblock. I just wish that van would turn up. You sure you don't want me to go with you and help hunt?"

"I think you'd be more useful here," Corbin replied with remarkable forbearance. "Officer Madigan should be along soon. You and she had better start going through your aunt's papers. See if you can get a lead on anybody who might have had a grudge against her, owed money they couldn't pay, or anything of that sort."

Shandy could tell Corbin was just putting up a decent pretense of making Flackley believe he wasn't being kept under surveillance, and he was sure the nephew realized it, too. However, Flackley seemed to be taking it well enough.

"Sure, I'll be glad to. Hey, did I hear you call this Madigan a she? Can she cook?"

"I wouldn't know about that," said Corbin, "but she's the best shot on the force and a black belt in judo. She also tends to be a bit touchy on the subject of female stereotypes. Maybe you'd better open a can of chili."

Flackley grinned. "Yeah, sounds like I better. You guys want some?"

"No, thanks. Here she comes now. We'll leave you to settle the lunch question between you."

A trim uniform and an air of brisk confidence suited Officer Madigan's svelte figure and pixie face to perfection. Frank Flackley looked a good deal brighter at the prospect of being left in her custody. Lieutenant Corbin gave Madigan a quick briefing, then he and Shandy took off.

They stopped to make inquiries at the few houses around Forgery Point, but got nothing of value. Nobody knew Martha Flackley's nephew was staying with her, but nobody seemed greatly surprised that he'd arrived. Flackleys had been going away and coming back for upward of two hundred years. They'd always been great ones for minding their own business, and they always seemed to have business to mind.

Martha Flackley had been a fine, honest, hard-working woman, not exactly popular but certainly well respected. Nobody could think of any reason why anybody would want to kill her. Nobody seemed to cherish any illusion that she'd be fool enough to keep valuables in the house. If she did, why choose such a complicated way to get at them when it would be easy enough to break in any day while she was off on her rounds?

Shandy was relieved when at last Corbin gave up and headed back toward Balaclava Junction. The state policeman refused his offer to stop at the brick house for potluck, which was just as well because Helen and Iduna turned out to be waist-deep in frying doughnuts.

"Good lord!" Shandy exclaimed. "What are we running here, a Salvation Army shelter? How many are you planning to feed?"

Helen scooped a crispy round out of the seething kettle

and laid it carefully on the draining rack. "So far we've had thirty-seven."

"Thirty-seven what?"

"People wanting to know if anybody else has found Belinda. We're handing out coffee and doughnuts to shut them up and keep them hunting. Want one?"

"I'd rather have a sandwich, if you don't mind. Anything but ham."

"Oh, Peter, haven't you eaten?"

"Not since breakfast, whenever that was. No, don't stop frying. I'll find something."

He poured himself a mug of coffee from the thirty-cup urn they'd set up on the kitchen table and foraged in the refrigerator for bread and cheese.

"This will do fine. Has Stott been by?"

"Twice so far. That man is distraught, Peter. He's out tearing up and down the back roads in that old Buick of his, checking on the search parties then rushing back to see if we've had any word from you. If it weren't for Iduna's doughnuts, he'd be a basket case by now."

The comely guest turned a fresh batch of dough out of the mixing bowl and began flattening it out on the floured breadboard with deft jabs of her rolling pin. "Can't blame the poor man for worrying. I'm concerned myself, and I've never even met her."

"You'd like Belinda," Helen assured her. "She's a lovely pig."

"I like most pigs."

Iduna had got the dough rolled out to the proper thickness and was popping the doughnut cutter up and down so fast it sounded like a tap dance.

"The only pig I never took to was an old gray hog my Aunt Astrid and Uncle Olaf used to have when I was little. Their pigpen was built right onto the outhouse, and as soon as he heard you open the door, that hog would start jumping up against the wall, making as if he was coming right in there after you. Aunt Astrid used to have to go with me and read me the Sears Roebuck catalog so I wouldn't be too scared to do what I went for. Do you want me to take over at the kettle for a while, Helen?"

"No, I think we'll finish this batch and call it quits. Why don't you sit down and have a cup of coffee with Peter? You've been working your head off ever since you got up."

"You don't call this work?" said Iduna. "I love to cook. Besides, we had that nice drive down to the supermarket."

"And a nice chat with Lorene McSpee while we were there," sniffed her hostess. "Honestly, Peter, that woman's a mental case."

"Never saw anybody buy so much bleach water at one time in my life," Iduna amplified.

"And she had two big bottles of that pine stuff you scrub floors with," Helen went on, "and a jug of ammonia. We couldn't help noticing. She plunked her carriage right in front of ours and started bombarding us with questions. So then I had to introduce Iduna, and then she had to know where Iduna came from and what she was doing here and how long she was going to stay and a good many other things that were none of her business. And then of course she got started on Miss Flackley."

"And then," chuckled Iduna, "I asked Mrs. McSpee if she was starting her spring cleaning. That wasn't much help."

"It was a perfectly natural thing to ask," Helen said, her blue eyes crackling in annoyance at Lorene McSpee. "Peter, you would not believe the earful she gave us about how it was going to take her another month's solid scrubbing to make the place livable. You know as well as I do that Mrs. Lomax and I went through Tim's house like a dose of salts, and we'd been dropping in every week to wash up the dishes and whatnot. Either that McSpee woman was trying to get my goat, which she certainly succeeded in doing, or else she's plain batty."

"It could be a little of both," said Iduna. "It does seem a shame, a nice man like Professor Ames having to put up with a pain in the neck like her. It's not on account of her red hair, either, no matter what they say. My Aunt Astrid had hair as red as a fox's tail and she was the loveliest woman you'd ever want to meet. She always had a kind word for everybody and a handout for any poor tramp that came along."

"Speaking of tramps," said Shandy, "I gather Tim's been over here?"

"Oh yes," said Helen, "he wandered along, wondering what the commotion was all about. He'd forgotten to hook up, as usual."

Professor Ames's daughter had strong-armed him into

getting a properly fitted hearing aid, but he seldom remembered to turn it on.

"Now, there's a man could use a little smartening up," said Iduna. "I'm surprised Mrs. McSpee doesn't use up a little of her energy mending his jacket. He's nice, though, isn't he? He showed me a whole pocketful of snapshots of his new grandchild. I love babies."

"Then you and Tim must get to know each other better," said Shandy, flashing a glance of triumph at Helen. "Timothy Ames is much too fine a man to be saddled with that pest of a housekeeper. What he needs—"

As he was warming up to a good, broad hint, the knocker sounded. Helen sighed.

"There's our thirty-eighth. Peter, would you answer the door? I'm all over doughnut grease."

Shandy obeyed. On the doorstep stood Professor Stott. His eyes were red and bleary, his clothing disheveled. Though the man could hardly have lost any appreciable amount of weight in so short a time, he somehow gave the impression of being gaunt and hollow-cheeked.

"Shandy," he blurted, "they've found the van."

"And Belinda?"

Stott groaned and shook his head. "On the seat was a ham salad sandwich. With a bite out of it!"

He collapsed into the nearest chair and buried his face in his hands.

"Shandy, what am I going to do?"

All Shandy could think of was to give him a slap on the shoulder. "Come on, old friend, the fight's not over yet. How about a drink?"

The only reply was a moan. Shandy went for a glass.

"It's Stott," he told the women. "They've found the van."

"Was Belinda in it?" asked Helen.

"No. Just a ham salad sandwich."

Iduna wiped her hands on her apron. "Where's the brandy, Helen?"

"Right here. Ask him if he wants a doughnut."

"Hot soup, quick."

Snatching the bottle and a tumbler, Iduna made for the front hall. Helen began to open a can of chicken noodle soup. Her husband shook his head.

"Helen, can you tell me how that woman has managed to escape matrimony all these years?"

"Just lucky, I guess."

His wife dumped the soup into a saucepan, set it over the fire, and gave him a rather slippery hug. "Peter, do you think that sow is alive?"

He rubbed her back. "I'm inclined to say yes. Surely the pignappers must realize Belinda's worth a great deal more as a breeder than as a barbecue. I expect a ransom note will be along as soon as they run out of nasty jokes."

"But why do they keep going through this obscene rigmarole with pigs' feet and ham sandwiches? They can hardly pretend it's all a jolly prank now that Miss Flackley's body has been found."

"Unless whoever's tending the pig doesn't know about the murder," Shandy mused. "God knows how many people were involved. It's possible the last one out killed her without telling the others and they've gone ahead with their plans out of sheer ignorance."

"Like Tom the Piper's son," said Helen. "I've always suspected it was Tom's father who ate that pig, then whipped Tom for stealing it. I'll bet whoever killed Miss Flackley will turn all mealymouth righteous and try to dump the blame on everyone else."

"Very likely," said Shandy. "Why should there be honor among pignappers? How's the soup coming?"

"Ready, I think. Bowl or mug?"

"Mug, by all means. I don't think he's up to lifting a spoon. That man's in rough shape, Helen. Do you think it's reasonable for him to be taking this thing so almighty hard?"

"You know him better than I do, Peter. The most likely explanation for his behavior is one I'm sure you don't want to hear."

"If you mean that Stott killed Miss Flackley, then rigged this scene with Belinda to cover up, I certainly don't," said her husband crossly. "Give me that soup."

Chapter 7

After he'd got some brandy and hot soup into him, Stott brightened a little.

"Thank you. You are friends indeed. I must go back."

"I'll go with you," said Shandy. "I'd like to see that van for myself. Are you sure your sow had been in it?"

"There was evidence," Stott replied with delicacy. "Belinda must have been under intolerable stress. She is fastidious in her habits, as a rule."

"Helen says she's a lovely pig," said Iduna. "I'm looking forward to meeting her."

"Miss Bjorklund, you give me heart."

Stott wrung the dimpled hand she held out to him after having given it a careful extra wipe on her apron, for Iduna, too, was fastidious in her habits. Then the two men went out to the Buick, which had been the Stott family conveyance ever since Shandy could remember.

They wound through the back roads into the foothills of Old Bareface. The mountain road was a lonely one, not much traveled except during autumn foliage time, when the leaf-lookers lined up bumper to bumper to view their Creator's handiwork and anathematize their fellow drivers. There were still patches of ice in the shadier places, yet Stott drove with reckless abandon, often exceeding the thirty-mile-an-hour speed limit and frequently failing to obey posted admonishments about falling rocks and deer crossings. Shandy sat trying not to grind his teeth, wondering why anybody would bring a pregnant sow up here.

For ditching a no longer wanted van, of course, the site was ideal. For concealing and maintaining a valuable animal the size of Belinda, it made no sense whatever. There were no cutoffs for miles either way. From now until the case was closed, the police would blockade both ends, interrogating every driver who came along and checking by radio to make sure he came out the opposite side within a reasonable length of time. Anybody who brought the creature to this Godforsaken place would have to be either remarkably stupid or totally indifferent to her survival. But what would be the point of bringing her up here to die?

What was the point of stewing about what the point might be until he'd learned something that bore at least a fleeting resemblance to a clue? Shandy had had approximately four hours' sleep after a day the like of which he'd hoped never to put in again, and now here he was in the midst of another mess. He leaned his head against the musty plush of the seat back and tried to doze.

The car stopped with a jolt. Shandy jerked upright. "Where are we?"

"This used to be a dirt logging road," Stott told him. "Some of the students had the perspicacity to search here. I believe the spot is not unknown to them."

"I believe I can guess why," grunted Shandy. "Where's the van?"

"Just beyond that clump of fallen timber." Stott clambered from behind the wheel and led the way.

The van was there, all right, surrounded by a bevy of police experts and a few members of the press who were being kept at bay by Fred Ottermole and his deputy. Ottermole greeted Shandy with the ease of old comradeship.

"Oh, Jesus, Professor, you here again? I might o' known. What the hell did you serve at that supper o' yours?"

"Remind me to invite you sometime, Ottermole," Shandy replied. "What have they found in the van?"

"Nothin' you folks couldn't use down at the gas plant. Been feedin' her some o' them turnips of yours?"

Ottermole was referring to the methane gas plant that provided power for Balaclava College and many of the surrounding houses, and was run solely on by-products from the digestive processes of Odin, Thor, Loki, Freya,

Balder, Tyr, Heimdallr, Hoenir, and the multitude of
other livestock that comprised the college herds. The turnip he mentioned so lightly was of course not *Brassica
rapa* but *Brassica napobrassica balaclaviensis,* commonly
known as the Balaclava Buster, that rutabaga whose su-
perior size, flavor and texture were relished alike by man
and beast and contributed in no small measure to the
generation of the gas that drove the turbines that lighted
the homes and heated the water and ran the electric
toothbrushes, hair curlers, shaving cream warmers, yogurt
manufacturers, weenie broilers, and other necessities of
modern civilization for the folk of Balaclava.

Because of its eagerness to flourish in cold climates,
the Buster played a not unimportant part in the economies
of Canada, Britain, the Baltic states, Sweden, Norway,
and even parts of Outer Mongolia, bringing sizable reve-
nues to Shandy and Ames, its developers, and Balaclava
College, its sponsor. It is said that prophets and rutabaga
breeders are not without honor save in their own baili-
wicks. The name of Shandy was revered in Riga and
honored in Oslo; on campus, the students called him Root.

Only behind his back, though. Professor Shandy, although neither dashingly young nor venerably old, neither
devastatingly handsome nor intriguingly ugly, neither
faster than a speeding freight train nor able to leap tall
buildings at a single bound, was nevertheless a man on the
tail of whose coat none but the most foolhardy cared to
tread. Nobody quite knew why. It was simply an accepted fact that Shandy was one faculty member you
didn't try to mess around with. Ottermole might venture a
joke, but when Shandy approached the van, the chief
didn't try to head him off.

"No clues, eh?" he remarked to one of the police
investigators who were going over the vehicle.

"No, just a few seeds. I suppose they were brought
along to feed the pig."

"May I see them?"

The man held out a folded paper.

"But these are sunflower seeds," Shandy objected.

"So?"

"You wouldn't feed sunflower seeds to a pig. They're
expensive, for one thing. Besides, they have hulls that
must be cracked before the meat can be got at, like pista-
chio nuts."

"Couldn't the pig chew up the seeds and spit out the hulls?"

"No doubt she could," said Shandy testily, "but why should she? There are lots of cheaper and more suitable things you can feed a pig. Where did you find these sunflower seeds"

"I told you, in the van."

"But what part of the van? Front or back?"

"Front," said the man rather sulkily. "Some on the driver's seat, some on the floor in the general vicinity of the gearshift."

"And how many are there?"

"How the hell do I know?"

Shandy was already counting. "Twenty-three, twenty-four, twenty-five, twenty-six. Are these all you found?"

"Yes."

"You're positive? None in the back?"

"No, there were none there."

"Any on the ground?"

"Gosh, I never thought to look."

"Then I suggest you do so now."

Stott, who had been waylaid by the reporter from the *Balaclava County Weekly Fane and Pennon,* now managed to get free and join Shandy.

Showing the folded paper, Shandy asked him, "Can you think of any earthly reason why anybody would feed Belinda sunflower seeds?"

The hog expert cogitated, then shook his massive head from side to side. "No reason. I do not believe Belinda would relish sunflower seeds. I am inclined to think Belinda would summarily reject sunflower seeds."

"Then how would you account for the presence of sunflower seeds in the van?"

"I should assume Miss Flackley was in the habit of feeding wild birds. Seeds of the *helianthus* are much esteemed, notably by the *paridae* and the *fringillidae.*"

"I'm a titmouse man, myself," said the officer wickedly. "So that's your answer, eh?"

"No, sir," said Stott, "that is merely my personal hypothesis. Many alternative explanations are equally possible. As an example, Miss Flackley may have been starting sunflower plants in a cold frame or greenhouse for later transplanting. Professor Shandy could speak with greater authority than I on that supposition."

Professor Shandy could, but he didn't want to. The notion of Miss Flackley's strewing birdseed around the cab of her van for any reason whatever might as well be rejected out of hand. Tim Ames would strew birdseed. He himself might happen to have a pocketful of seeds, as he often did, and possibly drop one or two while his mind was occupied by weightier matters. But Miss Flackley wouldn't. If she had for any reason been carrying sunflower seed around, she'd have had it stored in a spillproof sunflower seed container. If she happened to drop a single seed, she'd have picked it up. Ergo, as Stott would no doubt get around to saying sooner or later, those twenty-six sunflower seeds had not been spilled by Miss Flackley.

Nor would they have been left in the van by Frank Flackley, assuming a former rodeo worker was accustomed to carrying such things about on his person, because if he had been flinging them about with reckless abandon while she was driving him back to the house, she'd surely have taken time to sweep them out after he'd been left at home with his TV and six-pack. The almost inescapable inference was that they'd been spilled by the pignappers, and since it was extremely doubtful that anybody engaged in so fell a deed would be concerned with titmice, cardinals and goldfinches, it looked as if the driver himself had been nibbling on them en route to Old Bareface.

Himself or herself. Therein lay the rub. Among the student body there was in fact a small group apt to be carrying sunflower seeds and spitting the husks about the campus as a propaganda measure. These were the Vigilant Vegetarians.

Balaclava Agricultural College had always been a bastion of that gravely endangered species, the Independent Farmer. On the subject of cruelty to farm animals, it had taken a particularly militant stand, from the time when its founder, Balaclava Buggins, first inveighed against the overloading of draft animals down to present outcries from faculty and students alike against overcrowding and other gross malpractices of certain modern growers.

No alumnus of the Class of '73 would ever forget that electric moment when Thorkjeld Svenson in his Commencement remarks clove a solid oak podium neatly in twain from top to base as he slammed down his fist to emphasize those deathless words, "Agri isn't a business, it's a culture!"

As a farmer's highest calling was to serve the earth, but to be merry withal in his labor, so was a hog entitled to its wallow in good, soft mud and a cow to its cud of sweet, fresh grass beneath a shady tree before each fulfilled its ultimate destiny. No fowl went from incubator to coop to stewpot without ever once getting its claws in real dirt to scratch up its own worms.

No student could fault the care given the livestock, but some jibed at what happened when the care was ended.

There were several reasons why a student might become a vegetarian at Balaclava. For one thing, vegetarianism happened to be something of a national fad at the moment. For another, fresh milk, cheese, and eggs were available in any desired quantity; fresh vegetables abundant, varied, and extremely good. For a third, many young people don't much like meat anyway, and once they'd become personally acquainted with the college's cows, sheep, and swine, they particularly disliked the idea of meeting them at last in the form of roasts or chops. For a few, vegetarianism was a holy cause, and one of these was Birgit Svenson.

President Svenson and his wife, Sieglinde, had seven daughters, each, as a visiting professor from Dublin had once remarked, more beautiful than all the rest. The eldest four had been in their turns model students at Balaclava. One was a graduate student at Cornell now, three were married (the first to the visiting professor from Dublin), the two youngest were still in high school. All six of these had inherited their mother's serenity along with her loveliness. Birgit, the only one at present on the college rolls, had her mother's looks but her father's disposition.

Birgit's espousal of vegetarianism had been a stormy marriage from the outset. Her successful campaign to have soybean cutlets put on the menu in the student dining room had been only a warm-up skirmish for her battle to get roast beef and similar viands taken off. She and her cohorts armed themselves with statistics abut how many tons of grain it took to produce one ton of meat, and staged demonstrations at cattle shows where other Balaclava students were showing their prize Holsteins and Guernseys.

So far, the Viggies, as they had been dubbed, had succeeded in arousing considerable amusement, a certain amount of wholesome conscience-searching, and a few yelling matches; and a good deal of support for Oxfam and Care. Shandy suspected that Thorkjeld Svenson was privately amused by his firebrand daughter, and rather egged her on than otherwise.

The trouble with student activism, however, is that it may sometimes become hyperactive. During the past few weeks, Professor Stott had become the target for pointed attention. His obtaining large subsidies for his work in breeding meat animals was taken as a personal insult by a few of the more militant Viggies. While the rest of the student body was, as Moira Haskins had explained, making book on Belinda's progeny, Shandy had detected a few ominous murmurs among the anti-pork faction.

He himself, as an official ambassador to the vegetable kingdom, was apparently thought by some of the Viggies to be on their side. He had received veiled assurances that when the gravy started running in the gutters, his own giblets would be left intact. This would perhaps have been a comfort if he'd been inclined to take the matter with any degree of seriousness, but so far he hadn't, and suspected that almost none of the students had either, since there were so many other things on the fire, notably the Annual Competition.

Even Birgit Svenson was more interested in horses than their oats just now. Her own selected swain, one Hjalmar Olafssen, was the odds-on favorite to capture the Junior Plowmen's event, and had even received a bit of private coaching from Thorkjeld himself. Yet Svenson would expel Hjalmar without a second thought if he caught him up to any porcine hanky-panky, much less actual mayhem. Would the student jeopardize his chances at the Competition by engaging in such a stupid stunt as kidnapping Belinda of Balaclava?

He would if Birgit told him to. Moreover, if there was a way to botch up the operation, Hjalmar would be apt as not to find it. Although a master hand on the plow, a titan in the turnip field, and remarkable in a number of other areas, Hjalmar had his off moments. He was either incredibly brilliant or spectacularly inept at everything he

tackled, and nobody ever knew which would happen until it had irretrievably happened.

He was a straight A student in some subjects, a straight
F in others. Last year he had won top awards and almost
wrecked the bleachers when he stumbled clambering
down to collect them on prize-giving day. He had guided
his flock to a flawless first finish in the sheep-handling
trials, then tripped over Balaclava's Bruce of Bannock-
burn, the collie with whom he had been working. Bruce,
a sober and self-respecting animal, had been looking forward to another blue ribbon and a just meed of applause
for a job well done. When the collie bit Hjalmar, everyone realized he did it more in sorrow than in anger, but
the judges had to disqualify them anyway.

Hjalmar would be able to manage Belinda, of that
Shandy was quite sure. He was big enough and strong
enough, and had a way with animals. Even Bruce of Ban-
nockburn bore him no lasting grudge. Balthazar of Balaclava had been known to rouse from his slumbers and
waddle over to the side of his pen for the express purpose
of having his back scratched by Hjalmar. Any sow would
be putty in the student's hands.

Putty, perhaps, but never sausage. If Hjalmar had in
fact committed the incredible folly of letting himself get
mixed up in a pignapping, he would take care that no
harm came to the pig. Nor, for that matter, would he
wantonly have disarranged one tidy hair of Miss Martha
Flackley's head. The snag was that Hjalmar was so very,
very large, and that he had this ham-fisted streak in him.
Miss Flackley's mohair stole would be exactly the sort of
thing he couldn't go near without tripping over. Suppose
he'd crashed into her, and sent her reeling headlong
against the mash feeder? What would he do then? How
was it possible to know what Hjalmar would ever do at
any time?

Shandy tried to remind himself that Birgit and Hjalmar
were by no means the only ones involved in the Viggies
movement. At least a dozen other granola-breathing fire-
brands had tackled him only the previous week to see if
he would support their campaign to get research funds for
Professor Stott's projects shut off.

Birgit had not been among them. She at least had sense
enough to realize that Professor Shandy was not the sort
to stab a respected colleague in the back.

Neither had Hjalmar. The young man was not opposed to Stott's getting the money; he simply wanted the research directed into new channels, such as training pigs to be potato diggers, security guards, seeing-eye guides, and such, where their natural talents and sagacity could be utilized on a continuing basis rather than their natural succulence exploited as a one-shot deal. He had written a brilliant and persuasive paper on the subject. Professor Stott was said to be giving his arguments careful thought.

Knowing the rate at which Professor Stott's thought processes worked, though, Hjalmar might have reasoned that a little gingering-up mightn't hurt. Perhaps he'd intended to keep Belinda in some secret place pending her confinement, train the piglets according to his own enlightened methods, then parade them through the campus bearing placards with the message, EDUCATION, NOT AS-SIMILATION.

Shandy was momentarily intrigued by the notion, then rejected it. Olafssen simply wouldn't have the time, for one thing. He was carrying a stiff academic schedule, doing an elaborate and potentially important research project of his own on cucumber scab, and participating in practically every extracurricular activity on campus, from chess to horseshoe pitching; not to mention fighting off rival claimants for the favor of Birgit Svenson, which in itself would be a full-time occupation for the average male.

But Hjalmar wouldn't have been attempting this alone; that was the crux of the matter. What if he had in fact bumped against Miss Flackley and thought he'd only knocked her out? Might not some other member of the party have said, "You go ahead and get the pig away. I'll attend to her," or words to that effect? What if the other student then realized Miss Flackley was dead and jumped to the erroneous conclusion that it would be a noble act to conceal Hjalmar's crime? The handsome senior was a hero of sorts around Balaclava, and he was also one on whom many were pinning their hopes of winning the Competition. It was not impossible to suppose that some other student would take such an insane risk to protect him from the consequences of what he'd done.

Especially if that student was a young woman who was not Birgit Svenson. It was well known that many females were eating their hearts out over Hjalmar, just as the males yearned in vain after Birgit. But there was the problem of Miss Flackley's cut throat. The female of the species might be deadlier than the male, as Kipling claimed, but would any of them go that far?

There must be some other explanation for the sunflower seeds. Unfortunately, Shandy could think of one. Professor Stott's compassionate interest in the *Paridae* and *Fringillidae* was well known and Professor Stott was an absent-minded sort of man. If one happened to have a pocketful of birdseed and a handkerchief about one's person, and if one should reach into the pocket to get the handkerchief to mop one's brow during a particularly harrowing adventure, one would be likelier than not to scatter a fair number, such as twenty-six, of the seeds over the seat and floor of the van without noticing what one was doing.

If one couldn't think straighter than this, one had better stop trying to think at all. Shandy got busy helping to search the area around the van. Nowhere did he or anybody else turn up any more sunflower seeds, nor did they find the imprints of Belinda's feet, much less the signs of rooting that would probably have been Belinda's first act on being released from the van. The inference was that wherever she had been taken out, it wasn't up here on Old Bareface, and since Shandy had already decided this would be an extremely silly place to keep a pig, he was no further along than he'd been before.

When the van had been thoroughly searched, photographed, fingerprinted, and whatnot, the question arose as to whether it should be impounded as evidence or returned to the frustrated farrier at Forgery Point. There was indeed a schedule posted in the cab. According to its timetable, Flackley should at this moment be over in Hoddersville, attending to several draft animals belonging to various members of the Headless Horsemen, who had all but nosed out the Balaclava Brigade last year and were bragging that they'd surely capture the trophy this time.

Shandy felt a mean satisfaction at their being thwarted, then his better nature asserted itself and he threw his weight on the side of getting the van back to Flackley, or at least making available to him such tools as were essential to his craft. Since most of the van's contents had been removed and dumped in a heap back at the pigpens, presumably by the pignappers, then checked for fingerprints and bloodstains and found wanting, therefore use-less as evidence, the state police agreed to strike a compromise. If the college would lend Flackley a van, they'd release the equipment.

Shandy took it upon himself to say they would and per-suaded Stott to drive him back to arrange the matter. On the way, he managed to bring the subject around to sun-flower seeds, turning out his own pockets in a semijocular way to see if he himself could have dropped them, al-though he knew perfectly well he hadn't, and getting Stott to stop the car and do the same.

Stott cooperated without hesitation, surveying with gen-tle wonderment the agglomeration of articles he had been carrying around, but finding no sunflower seeds. That ruled out the possibility that he himself had inadvertently spilled them when he'd visited the van after it was first found.

It did not obviate the possibility that Stott had spilled them last night, though, because he'd been wearing dif-ferent clothes then. Why in Sam Hill couldn't Shandy think of a suspect who was somebody he didn't like?

Chapter 8

By the time Shandy had talked the superintendent of buildings and grounds into lending a van, got Flackley's tools and equipment loaded into it, and driven the vehicle out to Forgery Point with Helen following in their own car so he'd have transportation home, the farrier appeared to have lost his former zeal to snatch up the fallen torch.

He and Officer Madigan had made themselves snug in front of an open fire, with a card table set up and a game of gin rummy well under way. Various mugs, plates, and empty glasses showed they hadn't lacked for refreshment. Officer Madigan had removed her uniform jacket and looked flushed and rosy, no doubt from the heat of the fire; also a trifle vexed at being interrupted in the performance of her duty.

Shandy hadn't noticed before, but Frank Flackley was what he supposed some women would consider a reasonably good-looking man. He must ask Helen about that when they got back out to the car. In any event, Flackley took the keys of the college van with a moderate amount of grace, and did not seem overwhelmingly chagrined when he saw the schedule and realized how many horses he'd disappointed that day. He merely remarked that he probably ought to call them up from somewhere and explain but the chances were they'd already heard about Aunt Martha on the news. Then Flackley cast a thoughtful eye back at the card table and Officer Madigan.

The day was, in fact, further spent than Shandy had

77

realized by the time he was back in his own comfortable car. It felt good to be alone with Helen. She drove as she did everything else, in a spirit of amused wonder, as though she'd embarked on a fascinating experience for the first time and found she was surprisingly good at it. After being trundled about in Stott's ancient leviathan and jolted in the van, Shandy was altogether content to sit passive and let her go on driving. He liked the way her small hands in their brown leather gloves gripped the wheel. There was nothing about her he did not like. After a while, however, the gloves stirred a thought he'd as soon not have been bothered with again.

"If you were a Viggie, you wouldn't wear those."

"Wear what?" she asked.

"Leather gloves."

"Oh." Helen pondered the matter for a moment. "No, I suppose I wouldn't. Whatever put that observation into your head?"

"Sunflower seeds."

"I see. That explains everything."

"Helen, I'm a tired man."

"I know you are, poor pet, and you shall have rest. If anybody comes poking jars of pickled pigs' feet at you tonight, they'll have me to contend with."

"Noble woman! But seriously, getting back to the Vigilant Vegetarians, what do you think of them?"

"How do I know what I think of them? I'm not sure I've ever thought of them at all. My grandfather, Deacon Marsh, always maintained that the Lord gave man the birds of the air and the beasts of the field for his use, and I suppose I took the preachment at face value. I don't honestly see what's so awful about an honest working woman's warming her hands with a pair of gloves made from the hide of an animal that has already contributed its high-grade protein to the betterment of the race, though naturally I wouldn't buy a fur coat and I think leghold traps are an abomination. How did we get started on the Viggies, anyway?"

"I told you, the sunflower seeds. They found twenty-six sunflower seeds in the cab of Miss Flackley's van."

"Peter, I do see what you mean. One does manage to collect the odd seed or two in one's cuff or wherever from filling the bird feeders, but twenty-six is a lot for someone as neat as Miss Flackley was, so it must have been the

pignappers. I can see them buying birdseed to feed the
pig because it would throw people off the scent—oh dear,
that's a strange choice of words—but why get sunflower seeds when cracked corn or millet would be so
much cheaper and more suitable? It does suggest somebody who has them around to munch on, doesn't it? Like
Matilda Gables, which of course is ridiculous."

"Matilda who? Why?"

"You know that cute little sophomore with eyeglasses
about twice the size of her face, who wears the T-shirt
that reads, 'He prayeth best who loveth best All creatures
great and small.' She leaves a trail of sunflower seeds
every time she comes into the library. I think she must
have a hole in her blue jeans."

"Why doesn't she sew it up?"

"Peter, Matilda is a Brain. She wouldn't know which
end of a needle you're supposed to thread. I can't imagine what she's doing at Balaclava in the first place. She
ought to be at Harvard or Oberlin, majoring in Old Norse
or Pure Mathematics."

Shandy nodded. "I know. I'm afraid she's here out of a
sense of dedication. She's the type to see herself as the
flaming spearhead of a brave new order."

"But, Peter, she's so tiny!"

"So was David as compared to Goliath, since we seem
to have got off on a Biblical turn. If this Gables kid is so
brainy, she could surely find a way to manage the pig, or
cohorts to manage for her. Whom does she hang out
with?"

"I can't think of anyone offhand. Matilda generally
studies by herself. She does tend to gaze worshipfully at
Hjalmar Olafssen, but who doesn't? I do, myself."

Shandy groaned. "I wish you hadn't mentioned that lad.
Tell me one thing, have you ever caught Olafssen gazing
worshipfully back?"

"At me? Of course not."

"The more fool he. I meant at Matilda."

Helen shook her head. "No, I shouldn't say worshipfully. He's pleasant to her, of course. Hjalmar's always
kind to everybody, and everything. I suppose that's how
he got caught up in this Vigilant Vegetarians thing, that
and Birgit. Peter, you weren't thinking—"

There was no use trying to keep anything from Helen.

Shandy told her what he'd been thinking, and she drove for a while in silence.

At last she said, "I hate to admit it, Peter, but I think you're more apt to be right about the Viggies than about Professor Stott. Not that any of them did it, mind you, but—"

"Of course they didn't, but—"

"Well, anyway, I'll see what I can find out. The students talk to me sometimes, you know. I suppose they'll be getting back in classes Monday, now that the van's been found."

"Why? Belinda hasn't."

"No, of course not. I'm just not thinking straight. Oh, Peter, what a ghastly mess!"

"Yes, I daresay by now your friend Iduna wishes she'd stuck with the tornado."

"Actually, I think Iduna's having the time of her life. When you called and told me to bring the car, Professor Stott and Tim Ames were both there showing her pictures of their grandchildren. She'd already seen Tim's, of course, but she didn't seem to mind seeing them again. Peter, did you know that Professor Stott has twenty-four grandchildren already, and two more on the way?"

"Making a total of twenty-six. Good God, Helen, you don't suppose Belinda's being used for some kind of ritual sacrifice by the Planned Parenthood League?"

"I think that's the likeliest solution you've come up with yet," she replied. "Peter, do try to relax and get your mind off this dreadful business for a little while."

"How in Sam Hill can I, with everybody badgering me right and left? I suppose Svenson will be yowling at the door by the time we get home, demanding to know why I haven't got the case wrapped up in a neat package with a bow on it. Helen, you don't honestly think there's the faintest ghost of a possibility that Birgit Svenson could be mixed up in it?"

"I don't know what to say, Peter. Those Svenson girls must have a difficult time, trying to maintain the fiction that they're ordinary mortals like the rest of us. Birgit might possibly go along with some ridiculous stunt just to prove she's really one of the gang, or something, then have it backfire on her. Especially if Hjalmar was involved, and you can bet that if one of them was, they both were."

"If she is, there'll be seventeen different kinds of hell to pay," sighed Shandy. "Helen, do you realize what it would mean to the Svensons if their own daughter got mixed up in a murder? What it would mean to the college?"

"I don't even want to think about that. Peter, there must be an alternative possibility. What about this nephew, for instance, cropping up out of nowhere just at the crucial moment and stepping into a comfortable situation? Who's to say he didn't kill his aunt?"

"Who, indeed? And who's to say how he got from Old Bareface back to Forgery Point once he'd ditched the van? Not to mention all those merry pranks with the pigs' feet and pork chops when he has neither a car nor a telephone out there."

"Well, I don't care. I'd just like to know if he got off that Greyhound bus when and where he claims he did, and whether he made the trip alone."

"And you shall, my love. That's a damned good thought. If the state police haven't already thought it, which I'm inclined to doubt, we'll get them checking on that little question as soon as we're back home. I expect Officer Madigan has been working Flackley over pretty thoroughly on the details of his past life, and so forth, this afternoon."

"Especially the and so forth," Helen retorted. "Did it strike you that he's an extremely attractive man?"

"It struck me that some women might think so," her husband replied somewhat waspishly. "What is this? First I find you've been clandestinely ogling Hjalmar Olafssen, and now you start touting the attractions of Frank the Farrier."

"I didn't say he attracted *me*. I only meant he happens to have that smoldering, sexy quality about him that one or two sadly undiscriminating members of my gender might misguidedly prefer to more sterling qualities. Speaking of sterling, I wonder if they've caught the Carlovingian Cracksmen yet."

"If they have, it'll be on the six o'clock news. Which, come to think of it, was over half an hour ago."

"Maybe we could catch a broadcast on the car radio," said Helen, "though it hardly seems worth the effort now. Isn't it odd how one's perspectives can change so fast?"

"Oh, I don't know. I still wouldn't mind watching them

being lowered slowly into a vat of boiling oil. By the way, is Iduna still frying doughnuts, or do you think she might be giving some thought to supper?"

"That's right, you poor man, you've hardly had anything to eat all day. I'm sure she'll have something ready and waiting. Iduna has a natural affinity for cooking stoves."

"So I've noticed. You say she was cozying it up with old Tim, eh?"

"No, darling. I said she was looking at his and Professor Stott's kiddie snapshots with equal and unfeigned delight."

"That must explain why she hasn't married. She has a heart like Browning's Last Duchess, too easily made glad. Any galoot with a handful of baby pictures can come along and sweep the previous applicant off the boards before he's had a chance to pop the question."

"Peter, if you weren't already married to me, would you marry Iduna?"

"What kind of idiotic question is that? How could I not be married to you?"

"That's not what I asked."

"Well, that's my answer and I'm sticking to it. What are we having?"

"How do I know? I'm not cooking it. I bought a roasting chicken and some veal cutlets and a leg of lamb and a pot roast this morning."

"Sounds reasonably adequate. Helen, you do believe I was talking garbage about the Viggies, don't you?"

"What I believe is that you're tired and hungry and probably going to turn grouchy if you don't get some food and rest soon. Close your eyes and make believe you're stretched out on the sofa at home, listening to Mozart."

"Why not Brahms?"

"See, I knew you were getting cantankerous and contentious. Never mind, it's not far now. We'll probably get home and find that Belinda has turned up with her chops and hocks intact, and that Miss Flackley's secret lover, who's one of the Headless Horsemen of Hoddersville, has confessed to a *crime passionel,* and that Iduna has made Swedish meatballs."

"And Heavenly harps are sounding," grunted Shandy. "Not that I'd put anything past that bunch of fiends in subhuman form from Hoddersville, at that. Did I ever tell you about the time they poured itching powder down the back of President Svenson's overalls just as he was about to start his furrow in the Senior Plowmen's event?"

"No, but I expect you'll get around to it sometime or other. What happened?"

"What would you expect? Old Thorkjeld won the event in a time which has never since been equaled, had Sieglinde hold up Odin's blanket tentwise while he stripped and took a bath in the Gideon J. Higgins Memorial Horse Trough. Then he wrapped the blanket around him like a kilt, went over to the Hoddersville crowd, grabbed them two by two, cracked their heads together, and heaved them into the manure pile behind the cow sheds. It was an impressive spectacle."

"I can imagine. What did Sieglinde do then?"

"Beamed with wifely pride as the crowd gave him a standing ovation, then made him wipe out the horse trough so the animals wouldn't get sick from drinking the itching powder."

"There's always something rather terrifying about true greatness, isn't there?" said Helen in awe. "Who but Sieglinde would have remembered to clean the horse tank?"

"There's something terrifying about feminine logic, too," said her husband. "Why don't you and Sieglinde get together and think up a foolproof way to get rid of Lorene McSpee so Iduna can see how pitifully in need of a good woman's love Tim is? You'd enjoy having her for a neighbor, wouldn't you?"

"Peter, you're not minding about my having invited Iduna here without asking you first, are you?"

"No, my dear, I have other things to mind about, even if I chose to mind her being here, which I don't. What I mind most is not being able to quit fretting about those students. Drat it, Helen, I'd have sworn we've as fine a lot here as you'd come across anywhere in the country. How could Birgit Svenson get herself mixed up in a thing like this?"

"Peter, you have no earthly reason to suppose Birgit is mixed up in anything at all. Now for goodness' sake, let's talk about something else for a change."

"What, for instance?"

"Well, the horse show. Shouldn't you be training for the oat-shucking contest or something?"

"There won't be one. It is not possible to shuck an oat. Oats don't have shucks."

"Then what do they have? Oh, I know, it's always in crossword puzzles. Awns. No, I suppose one couldn't very well hold an awning, could one?"

"Not over an oat, at any rate. At least I daresay one could and it's entirely possible somebody has, but it would seem a footling sort of activity. Why don't you look it up? If there are any statistics available, I suppose I ought to know about them."

"I'll do that, assuming I ever get back to work. Did you know that Dr. Porble closed the library today, for the first time in history, excluding national holidays and Balaclava Buggins's Birthday? He was out hunting the pig with the rest of them. Oh, I am sorry! We just can't get away from it, can we?"

"No, we can't, and what's the sense in trying?" sighed Shandy. "Well, the last mess I got stuck in, I wound up with you. That kind of luck couldn't happen twice, but I suppose it wouldn't hurt to hope for the best."

He didn't add, "while we're expecting the worst." He didn't have to.

Chapter 9

It was almost dark when they got back to the brick house. Helen was feeling guilty at having left Iduna for so long, but she needn't have. They found their guest comfortably settled in front of the television set communing with Walter Cronkite. She had changed into what Shandy's mother would perhaps have called a wrapper and Helen's a lounging costume. Whatever the thing was, it became her immensely. In her hand was a Balaclava Boomerang and on her face was a smile of sweet content.

"I didn't know when you folks would be along, so I rummaged around in the icebox and threw some things together. There was a canned ham I thought might go kind of nicely with those sweet potatoes we bought and wouldn't be hurt if it had to set awhile. I figured Peter would need something hearty after the day he's put in. It's all keeping hot in the oven anytime you've a mind to eat. I made myself one of those boomerangs of yours, Peter. Never thought I'd wind up a solitary drunkard."

"You won't," Shandy assured her, heading for the bar. "Same for you, Helen?"

"By all means," said his wife. "Iduna, I suppose I should make some hypocritical noise about how you shouldn't have gone to so much trouble, but I'm not going to. You've probably saved both our lives. When did Professor Stott and Professor Ames leave?"

"Oh, quite some time back. I've had all sorts of company since then. Young folks, mostly. There was one boy who reminded me of my cousin Margit's son Willem.

85

Handsome a chap as you'd ever want to lay eyes on, but
he couldn't take two steps without falling over his own
feet."

"Olafssen!" exclaimed Shandy. "What did he want?"

"Doughnuts. Leastways that's what he got. He mainly
wanted to talk to you, Peter, but he didn't say what
about."

"Drat! I wish I hadn't missed him. Did he say when
he'd be back?"

"Nope, just said he was going to hunt the pig some
more. I felt downright guilty fixing that ham, though I
reckon there's not much sense in that. If they weren't
good to eat people wouldn't raise them, and think of all
the fun they'd miss before they got eaten. That's what I
said to Professor Stott and he agreed with me. He *is* a
fine-looking man, isn't he? Sort of noble and majestic.
He reminds me of that prize boar the Knebels used to
have. You remember, Helen? He's got that same proud
way of looking you straight in the eye and flaring out his
nostrils. Why, thanks, Peter, I don't mind if I do, though
you'd better go a little easy on the applejack this time if
you want any supper tonight."

"But, Iduna, you're supposed to be our guest," Helen
protested. "You've already done more than your share.
We don't expect you to wait on us."

"Nonsense. Now that I've got to start earning my
keep, it won't hurt me to get in a little practice. Well, it
sure is an ill wind that blows no good, as I told Professor Stott. If that tornado hadn't come along, I wouldn't
be sitting here having the time of my life, though I expect I shouldn't say so with that nice Miss Flackley dead
and gone and Belinda still missing. But you never know,
that's what I told him. It's always darkest before the
dawn."

"You and Stott seem to have had quite a philosophical
discussion," Shandy grunted rather sourly. "How did
you get on with Tim?"

"Professor Ames? Oh, we managed fine once he remembered he was supposed to turn on that little switch.
But I'd keep my own earphones shut off if I had to listen to that Mrs. McSpee nagging me about wiping my
feet every time I turned around. She came over here looking for Professor Ames just before six o'clock because
she claimed she had his supper almost ready, but be-

tween you and me and the gatepost, I think it was no
more than an excuse to find out what was happening
over here. Anyway, she sat here talking for maybe ten
minutes, and I declare, if she'd stayed much longer I
might have said something I'd have been sorry for. Nag,
whine, fuss, complain, and such a smell of Clorox around
her you'd think she dabbed it behind her ears for per-
fume. I just plain don't see how that man stands her."

"What was she crabbing about this time?" asked Helen.

"Oh, things in general, but especially the murder.
She's got some bee in her bonnet that it was a maniac
who's going around killing lone women. I said to her,
'Why, Mrs. McSpee, you're not alone. You've got Professor Ames right there in the house with you,' and she
gave him a look as much as to say, 'What good would he
be?' I wanted to speak up and say she was safe because
not even a murderer could stand to get close enough to
kill her, but I managed to hold my tongue. I do think
that's an awful thing to do, though, ripping a man up the
back right in front of his own face. Don't you?"

Shandy choked on his drink. Helen gave him a look.
Though probably not so scathing a look as Lorene Mc-
Spee had given Timothy Ames, it had its effect. He
nodded his head in solemn agreement.

"You're absolutely right, Iduna. No excuse whatever
for her to make such a remark. If you needed a good
man in a tight place, you'd never do better than count on
Timothy Ames. Would she, Helen?"

"Peter, you know I'm hopelessly prejudiced about
who's the best man in these parts," Helen replied lightly.
"Now, I'm going to put the food on the table and you
two are going to sit here and enjoy your drinks till I call
you. Iduna, tell Peter about the time you and I decided
to enter a jar of watermelon pickles in the county fair."

Miss Bjorklund obligingly began some pleasant narrative, chuckling every so often at her own recollections.
Shandy chuckled, too, not because he was paying any attention to her story but because he wanted her to keep
talking. It was like having somebody sing him a lullaby.
He was almost asleep when Helen summoned them to
dinner, and ate his meal in an agreeable state of semi-
somnolence while his wife and her friend reminisced.

That was by far the pleasantest interlude of that long,
harrowing day. It lasted far too short a time. They had

finished wedges of a custard pie angels might have en-
vied, cleared away, and got themselves back to the fireplace when Mirelle Feldster blew in. As usual, she was in
the midst of a sentence before Helen could get the door
open. Without waiting to be asked, she flung her coat over
a chair and plunked herself down in the middle of the
sofa.

"So I expect it's only a matter of time before they arrest the brute. Nice bit of publicity, I don't think! Seems
to me we've been in the news entirely too often for comfort ever since Peter decided to get cute with those
Christmas trimmings of his."

"One thing I'll say for you, Mirelle, you certainly
know how to get the most out of a grudge," said Helen
with no particular rancor. "Who's going to be arrested,
and why?"

Mirelle's marshmallow features gathered themselves
into a series of bunches intended to express regret and
disapproval, but betraying only eagerness to spread the
news. "Why, Stott, of course, for murdering that Flackley woman."

"Well, that's the nuttiest thing I ever heard!"

Iduna blushed. "Sorry to be so plain-spoken. I don't
know who told you that piece of foolishness, but whoever it was better go get his mouth washed out with
brown laundry soap. Excuse me, Helen, I didn't mean to
butt in like this."

"Not at all, Iduna. You took the words right out of my
mouth. Oh, I beg your pardon, I don't think you two
have met. Mirelle Feldster, our next-door neighbor; Iduna
Bjorklund, an old friend of mine from South Dakota."

Mirelle wasn't a bit fazed. "We introduced ourselves
this afternoon. I stopped in to see if there'd been any
news about the pig. Jim wouldn't tell me anything, naturally, and now he's off to another of his lodge meetings."

Jim Feldster, a member of the animal husbandry
department, belonged to a number of fraternal organi-
zations. It seemed odd that he'd take off to attend any
such function at a time like this, but perhaps she went to
enlist the aid of his lodge brothers in the search. On the
other hand, perhaps he just couldn't face the thought of
an evening with Mirelle after the day he must have put
in. It was generally understood that Jim sought fraternity
as a relief from conjugality, and nobody blamed him

much, though his being gone so often had the unhappy effect of turning his wife loose on the community at large for her diversion. She was always the first to know everything, and the likeliest to get it wrong.

Nevertheless, her tongue could do harm, and often had done. Likely as not it was she herself who'd thought up this balderdash about Stott's getting arrested. The important thing was to squash her before she could spread the word around.

"Why, it's all over campus," she hedged. "As soon as people heard about your having the pair of them to dinner last night—"

"What?" cried Helen. "Why would anybody think anything of that?"

"Helen, dear," said Mirelle sweetly, "we may be hicks from the sticks compared to the clever sophisticates you used to know in all those other jobs you got fired from, but we're not quite the mental incompetents you seem to think we are. How did you ever manage to worm it out of them, after they'd managed to keep it quiet for so long?"

"Keep what quiet? Mirelle, do you have the remotest idea what you're talking about?"

"Why, about Stott and the Flackley woman, of course. To think of its going on year after year right under our noses, and her prissing around as if butter wouldn't melt in her mouth. I understand now there's some talk of exhuming Elizabeth Stott. I suppose Flackley figured after Elizabeth died he'd make an honest woman of her, but he let things drag on for fear of jeopardizing his position with Svenson. Then when you brought it out in the open the way you did, they had a big fight and—"

"Mirelle Feldster, you ought to be certified!"

Helen was blazing now. "Do you mean to sit here in my own house and tell me you've cooked up a big scandal out of nothing but the simple fact that I happened by the merest chance to invite two people to dinner on the same evening?"

"I'd hardly call it nothing, Helen. After all, the poor woman's dead. We might as well be charitable."

"Then your charity had better begin at home! I stopped to chat with Miss Flackley the other day while I was over looking around the animal husbandry barns. She struck me as an interesting woman and I invited her to dinner so that I could get to know her better. Professor Stott came along to look at his pig and stopped to say hello to us, so I asked him, too. Peter and I often do, as I'm sure you're aware, since he's alone at home and I enjoy his company. So does my husband, in case you're wondering."

"For that matter," said Iduna, casting a cold eye at Mirelle, "who wouldn't? I took to Professor Stott right away, myself."

"There, see," crowed Mirelle as if her point had been proved. "It's all right, Helen dear. I quite understand how upset you must be at getting your husband into another fix when he'd barely crawled out from under the last one. I simply thought I'd drop over and offer my sympathy for what it's worth, which doesn't seem to be much. I've got to run."

She picked up her coat and was gone before anybody could have the pleasure of slamming the door behind her. It was Iduna who found her voice first.

"Well," she said placidly, "can you beat that?"

"I'd like to," said Helen through clenched teeth. "Peter whatever happened to those ducking stools they used to have for scolds and gossips?"

"Good question. I'll bring it up at the next faculty meeting. Good God, Helen, do you realize she's probably spouted that filth to the police?"

"Of course she has, and Heaven only knows how much more. Iduna, I hate to say this, but by this time tomorrow that woman will have told at least thirty people about how Professor Stott murdered Miss Flackley so he could start a red-hot love affair with you."

"That'll be something to write the folks back home, won't it? Helen, why don't I go tidy up in the kitchen and give you and Peter a little time to yourselves? That silver of yours is so gorgeous it's an honor to wash it."

"Speaking of silver," Helen said to get the taste of Mirelle out of the air, "did you happen to hear anything about that robbery on the news?"

"They had an interview with a Mr. Birkenhead. The reporter asked him what the value of the gold and silver was, and he said as far as he was concerned, the main value of the metal lay not in its monetary cost but in the skill of the artisans who fashioned it. Therefore, he didn't consider his company to have been seriously affected by the robbery. I thought that was pretty classy, myself. Anyway, he wouldn't come right out and say how much those men stole, but it seems there was an extra lot of gold in the place just then because they're making a special dinner service for one of those Eastern potentates, so it's estimated they must have got at least half a million dollars' worth, all told."

"And to think I rode off in the van with it," said Helen in some awe.

"And to think I helped lug it out," said Shandy, pulling his wife closer to him. "Helen, do you think I'm some kind of Jonah?"

"No, but if you don't go easy on Iduna's cooking, you may turn into some kind of whale," she replied. "Peter, you're not going to let yourself be influenced by anything Mirelle Feldster said, are you? You know she's got scrambled eggs where her brains should be."

"Yes, I know. But it seems lately that— Oh, Christ, what now?"

The brass knocker was being thumped again, this time in a slow, reverberating knell. Shandy untangled himself from his wife and got up to answer the door. To his unconcealed amazement, the caller was Harry Goulson, Balaclava Junction's friendly neighborhood mortician.

"Good God!" was Shandy's suave and polished greeting.

"Nope, just the guy who comes to pick up the pieces afterward," Goulson replied cheerfully. He was a jolly soul with a quip for every occasion, except when engaged on professional business. "I was wondering if I could bother you for a few minutes, Professor?"

"Why not? Everybody else does. Come in, Goulson, take a pew. Forgive my abruptness just now. I was— er—surprised to see you because I thought you'd be at the lodge meeting with Jim Feldster. Mirelle was just here and she mentioned that he'd gone. Have you met my wife, by the way?"

"Evening, Mrs. Shandy. The pleasure's probably more mine than yours."

"Not at all," said Helen politely. "May I take your hat? Would you care for a cup of coffee?"

"Gosh, no, thanks. I just wanted a word with the Professor, here."

"Then I'll go help Iduna in the kitchen and leave you to it."

Helen left the room. Goulson took a straight chair and leaned forward, still wearing his good-quality black overcoat, still clutching his well-brushed black fedora.

"The thing is, Professor, Fred Ottermole tells me you're sort of the go-between on this awful thing that happened up here last night."

"President Svenson—er—appointed me in some such capacity, yes."

"Well, that's why I thought I'd come to you. To tell the honest truth, I didn't have nerve enough to tackle the President about this, but—well, I sort of thought you might understand."

"It's possible I might, if you'd care to explain," said Shandy rather pointedly.

Goulson drew in his breath. "The long and short of it is, I'd like to handle Martha Flackley's funeral."

"I don't know why you shouldn't. You're not exactly—er—pressed for competition around here, are you? However, I should think the proper person for you to speak to is Frank Flackley, the nephew who's staying at her house. He seems to be next of kin."

"Yes, but who is he?" said Goulson. "I mean, I know he's a Flackley and all, but he doesn't know me from a hole in the wall, and I don't even know which branch of the family he comes from. Now, with Martha it was different. I knew her father and my father before me knew his father before him, and that's the way it's been right down through the years. I'm not trying to claim the Goulsons and the Flackleys were ever what you'd call lodge buddies or anything like that, but what with old families dying off, we're the two longest-established family businesses in this neck of the woods and we've always had respect for one another.

"I was standing right there in the shed the day my father told Will Flackley he was buying a motorized hearse. 'Will,' he says, 'I can't tell you how bad I feel about this, but my clients expect it and I've got to move with the times. But I tell you what I'll do, Will, when your time comes, I'll see that you get a proper send-off with two good horses and the old high-sprung hearse, same as your father and your grandfather before him. And if I go before you, my son here will honor the promise. Won't you, Harry?' And I said, 'Yes, Pop,' and I meant it.

"Well, to make a long story short, we buried Will Flackley the way we said we would, and we didn't charge the family one cent for it, either. Father was still alive though failing then, and he sat on the seat with me while I handled the reins. That was the last time we used the old horse-drawn hearse, but I've kept her in the shed as a family heirloom and she's all shined up and ready to go tomorrow.

"What with modern progress and all, Martha and I never had any business dealings. We used to pass the time of day now and then when we'd happen to bump into each other, and she never forgot what we did for her father, but we both had our businesses to tend to and she was never one to mix in much. Be that as it may, she's got nobody left now except this foreigner out of God knows where, and I just figure it's up to me to see she gets a decent funeral. I'm not looking for any pay and I wouldn't take it if anybody offered. One of these days, the Lord willing, I'm going to meet Father on that bright and shining shore and I want to be able to walk up to him and say, 'Pop, I kept my promise.' I suppose that sounds crazy to you, eh?"

Shandy found it necessary to blow his nose before replying. "Not at all. Why should it? A man owes a duty to his profession."

"You hit it right on the button, Professor. Oh, I know folks call me Harry the Ghoul and make jokes about vampires and bloodsuckers and the rest of it. I'm not claiming we're all saints in my profession any more than they are in yours, if you'll forgive me for raking up what's better buried and forgotten, Balaclava Agricultural College being a fine old institution and a credit to the county ever since the time of Balaclava Buggins, may he rest in peace, as we say in the trade. The undertaking profession has had its share of crooks and fakers same as the institutes of higher learning, much as we try to keep them out, but I will say you won't find many morticians who won't at least put up a decent show of respect for the dead and compassion for the bereft at a time when it's most needed.

"A human body may be no more than a shell, as the preachers say, but it's a shell that's maybe come in mighty handy to somebody for a lot of years and it's entitled to proper handling when it's outlived its usefulness. I'd say Martha Flackley's been as useful as anybody, and I want her done right by. Well, there, I guess I've spoken my little piece, and now I'll take myself off."

Shandy got up to see him to the door. "If it's not an impertinence, Goulson, I'd like to say that I'm honored you've shared your feelings with me. I'll explain to young Flackley, who I'm sure will be both relieved and gratified, and I'll also find out from the state police when you can—er—get on with it. Was that what you wanted?"

Goulson fiddled with his black fedora. "As a matter of fact, there was one other thing. You see, we don't have any horses to draw the hearse. I could maybe talk to some of the boys from Hoddersville or Lumpkin Corners—"

"Never!" said his host. "I'll tell President Svenson you need two Balaclava Blacks, and I think I can safely promise you'll get them, though I feel it my duty to warn you that he may insist on driving them himself."

"Heck, he's welcome as the flowers in May, and I'm sure Martha would feel the same. Thanks a lot, Professor."

"Not at all. You understand, of course, that the funeral would have to be held on a day that wouldn't interfere with the Competition."

"Naturally. Wouldn't be anybody left in town to come to it anyway, would there? Think we're going to take the cup again this year?"

"We're going to give it the old school try, at any rate. Thanks for dropping by, Goulson. Here, let me get that door for you."

With a certain amount of handshaking and shoulder slapping, the two men parted. A moment later, Helen was at her husband's side.

"What was that in aid of?"

"It was a powerful lesson in the folly of pinning labels on one's fellow humans," said Shandy. "Helen, if you ever hear me refer to that man as Harry the Ghoul again, I hope you'll do me a big favor and punch me square in the mouth."

Chapter 10

"Well, naturally, your wish is my command," said Helen. "I'll bop you anytime you give the word, but would you care to explain why?"

Before Shandy could do so the knocker sounded again. "Drat!" he exploded. "This is getting to be like one of those farces where people keep popping in and out."

"That's the way it's been all day long," Helen sighed. "I'll go."

Oddly enough, this caller was one Shandy didn't mind seeing, since it meant he could clear up Goulson's business forthwith. Frank Flackley stood there looking like a sheepish cowboy who'd come to town to mingle with the swells, which may have been how he felt.

"I couldn't find a couple of things that ought to have been in Aunt Martha's van and thought they might have left'em back there at the pigpens," he explained, "so I took a run down to see if I could find'em. Thought I might as well drop in and say thanks for all you did, Professor, borrowing me that van from the school and getting my tools for me. Looks like Flackley the Farrier will be back in business tomorrow for sure."

He grinned and slipped off the jacket Helen was offering to take from him. "Thanks, ma'am, that's kind of you. I guess you must have thought I wasn't very grateful back there at the house, after you going to so much trouble. See, it was sort of—oh, I don't know—discouraging, I guess you might say, when they wouldn't give me back the Flackley van. I mean, I'd got myself all fired up to take over the family business, and now it's like as if I was starting on any new job that happened along. I guess you folks ain't much interested in hearing my problems."

"Of course we are," Helen said graciously. "Sit down and let me get you a cup of coffee and a piece of pie."

"Or a drink, if you'd rather," said Shandy. "As a matter of fact, you came at the perfect time. I have something to discuss with you, and this will save my having to hunt you up tomorrow. Scotch? Bourbon?"

"Beer, thanks, if you got it. What did you have in mind, Professor?"

"Wait a second, I want my wife to hear this, too. I was about to tell her when you arrived."

Helen was soon back, bringing a tray with a bottle of beer, one of brandy, and some glasses of appropriate sizes. Iduna followed, bearing a plate of crackers and cheese. At sight of her, Flackley rose from the chair he'd just taken and perked up a good deal.

"Happy to meet you, Miss Bjorklund," he said when introductions had been duly performed. There was no doubt in anyone's mind that he meant what he said.

"So you're from the wide-open spaces, like me. We played South Dakota a few times, but to tell you the truth, I forget just where we was at. After a while you get so all them little towns look alike to you. Don't s'pose you ever happened to catch our show, Rudy's Rough Riders?"

Iduna shook her head until the golden curls seemed to shoot out baby sunbeams. "No, I never did. But I'm sure you took lovely care of those poor animals."

"I done my bit. Are you going to be here long?"

Flackley did a neat bit of footwork and got himself seated on the sofa next to Iduna. Gallantly he raised his glass of beer and clicked it against the infinitesimal tot of brandy she'd allowed herself.

"Here's looking at you."

"And that's no idle statement," Helen murmured to Peter, as she handed him his brandy. "Is that enough for you, dear?" she added in a normal tone.

"Plenty, thanks. Flackley, what happened to Officer Madigan?" he couldn't resist asking.

The bearded man grinned, quite unabashed. "Oh, she got relieved from duty. I guess the fuzz checked me out and found out I was no more than what I claimed to be, so they called off the bloodhounds. I don't blame'em for being suspicious, a roughneck like me coming out of nowhere, as you might say, just when Aunt Martha—" his voice faded.

"Mr. Flackley, I just can't tell you how awful we feel about your aunt," Iduna put in. "To think that last night this time she was sitting right where you are now!"

Flackley shifted as if the idea made him uncomfortable, but somehow managed to wind up closer to Iduna. "Yeah, I guess I still haven't quite taken it in. I didn't even know Aunt Martha till I got here. I guess she and my folks used to write back and forth sometimes, but you know how kids are, I never paid no attention. Then I struck out on my own, and then my folks died and I just sort of lost track of the family till the rodeo busted up and I took this notion to come back east. You have to admit it looks sort of funny, me coming here just when I did, and if you was to ask me why I done it, I couldn't tell you. It plain hit me between the eyes, I got to go back, and I got on the bus and come. Almost as if it was meant to be, or somethin'. Not that I take any stock in that kind of stuff," he added hastily.

"You're right about Aunt Martha bein' a lovely lady, though. I *am* goin' to miss her. I been a rolling stone too long."

He inched yet closer. "That's a real nice house, out there at Forgery Point, but it gets lonesome in the evenings with nobody around. To tell you the plain truth, I didn't really have to come down here after them tools tonight, I just couldn't stand sitting there by myself thinkin' about what happened. Not that I didn't mean what I said about being grateful to you, Professor."

"Of course," said Shandy, "I understand. While we're on the subject of your aunt, I suppose I might as well get our bit of business off my chest. It's about Miss Flackley's funeral."

"Oh yeah. I been wonderin' what I ought to do about that."

"That's what I wanted to tell you. Actually, you don't have to do anything whatever. Our local undertaker, Harry Goulson, was here not fifteen minutes ago, offering to handle the whole thing at no charge to you or to her estate."

"Huh? How come?"

"Essentially because the Goulsons have always buried the Flackleys, and he promised his father he'd continue the old custom. Goulson wants to use the old horse-drawn hearse that was last used for her father's funeral. I think it's damned decent of the man," Shandy added in rather a fierce tone.

"Yeah," Flackley replied thoughtfully. "Yeah, it sure is. You mean the whole thing, coffin, flowers, and all?"

"So I gathered. If I may say so, I think you couldn't do better than take Goulson up on his offer and trust him to do everything the way your Aunt Martha would have wanted it."

"This Goulson, what sort of a guy is he?"

"One of the best."

"I meant is he old, young, middle-aged? Good-looker? Snappy dresser? Smooth line of talk?"

Shandy rubbed his chin. "As to age, I'd say he was more or less a contemporary of your aunt. He has an agreeable appearance and personality. Wouldn't you say so, Helen?"

"Mr. Goulson is a very pleasant man. Everyone seems to like him. Being a snappy dresser wouldn't be exactly appropriate in a man of his profession, but he always looks presentable."

"Married, I suppose?"

"Yes, and a grandfather several times over. I'm slightly acquainted with his wife. She's president of the garden club."

"I figured. Well, what do you know?"

The question seemed to be rhetorical. Flackley stared into the fire for some moments without speaking. Then he said softly, "There had to be some reason why she stayed single all her life. Aunt Martha must have been real pretty when she was young. What the heck, no reason for me to pass judgment, is there?"

"I don't think I follow you, Flackley," said Shandy in that special tone of voice his students strove to avoid hearing.

"Well, Professor, seems plain enough to me. What would you think if you was in my place?"

"I'd think a decent man was trying to do a decent thing."

"Isn't that just what I'm trying to say? Sure, Professor, you can tell this Mr. Goulson I'd be much obliged and

for him to let me know what he wants me to do when
the time comes. I guess he'll know how to go about the
paper work, or whatever. The police have got her now,
haven't they?"

"Yes, they have. I'll explain the matter to them in the
morning and let Goulson take it from there."

"That's mighty nice of you, Professor. I appreciate it.
Look, I better be gettin' back. I'd hate to be lost among
them Seven Forks late at night. Thanks for the beer, Miz
Shandy. And it sure was nice meetin' you, Miss Bjorklund. Be seein' you again, I hope."

"I shouldn't be surprised."

Iduna gave her dimpled hand in farewell and it was a
moot question whether Flackley meant to give it back.
Eventually, however, he wrenched himself free, buttoned
up the handsome leather jacket he'd worn against the chill
of the night, and went out to the borrowed van.

"What was he trying to get at about Miss Flackley's
having had an affair with Goulson?" Shandy sputtered.

"Stranger things have happened," said his wife,
"though personally I can't envision a lover's embalming
his old sweetheart as a farewell gesture."

"It wouldn't seem right somehow," Iduna added.

"No, it damned well wouldn't, and I don't believe it. I
only hope Flackley doesn't go sprinkling hints around."

"Where would he sprinkle them?" said Helen. "He
doesn't know anybody in this area."

"How long do you think it's going to take that chap to
get acquainted?"

"He does seem a friendly type," she agreed. "Iduna,
I have a sneaky feeling you've just acquired another
fan. Think you could settle a roving cowboy?"

"I've settled a few in my time," the guest replied with
a saucy toss of her curls. "Well, if you'll excuse me, I
think I'm ready to call it a day."

"I move we all turn in before anybody else decides to
come visiting," said Helen. "Give me that tray, Iduna,
and go on upstairs. You deserve the bathroom first after
the work you've done. At least I'm glad Flackley didn't
make any fuss about the funeral. Personally I think it's a
lovely thing for Mr. Goulson to do."

"So do I, and I can't see why Flackley couldn't accept
it as such. I'm going to see the President first thing in the
morning about the horses."

"I think Miss Flackley would have liked one of them to be Loki," said Helen. "She had a special soft spot for him, I believe."

"Helen, you appear to be the only person in the world who knew anything at all about Miss Flackley, and you only met her a couple of days ago."

"Yes, and it positively breaks my heart that I'll never get a chance to know her any better. Oh, Peter, such a dreadful waste of a genuinely good life! Honestly, I've never thought of myself as a vindictive woman, but if I ever got my hands on whoever stuffed her into that mash feeder, I'd—well, I don't know what I'd do, but it would be something I'd no doubt be ashamed of for the rest of my life, so I hope I never get the chance. Give me a kiss and let's go to bed. I need to get my mind on something pleasant for a change."

Chapter 11

The following morning, Shandy slept a good deal longer than he'd meant to. A smell of fresh-brewed coffee and a sound of gentle womanly voices from belowstairs gave him a sense of well-being until he recalled that his first duty of the day must be to beard Thorkjeld Svenson on the delicate subject of Goulson's using the college horses, and that his next would no doubt be at least equally obnoxious.

He got up and went to the window for the innocent purpose of seeing what sort of day it was, and his eye alit on two ladies in earnest conference down in the Crescent. They were Lorene McSpee and Mirelle Feldster. At that point, he pondered the wisdom of going back to bed and hiding under the covers, but Shandy was no poltroon. He shaved, took a shower, put on a plaid shirt of somber hues and a pair of work pants, and went to face whatever must be faced.

As his first encounter was with his wife and his second with Iduna's radiant smile, he began to perk up. The pair of them led him to the breakfast table and began to heap bounty upon him.

"How about some pancakes?" Iduna suggested.

"Oh, don't bother for me."

"It's no bother. We mixed them up for Professor Stott, and there's plenty of batter left over."

"Stott was here and you have leftovers? Good Gad, the man must be falling apart!"

"Peter, he is," said Helen. "It's heartrending. He's been

out since before dawn hunting for Belinda. I don't know what's going to happen to that man if she doesn't turn up soon."

"Are the students out again?"

"In force. He's got them organized into platoons and squadrons and I don't know what all, armed with geodetic survey maps and under orders to leave no stone unturned. It simply doesn't seem possible she could be far away, considering the short span of time the pignappers had to work in. We know Miss Flackley couldn't have been killed much before midnight because she was with us, and it was only about four hours later that Professor Stott showed up brandishing that jar of pigs' feet."

Shandy speared a piece of pancake. "And by then he'd spent a certain amount of time dithering about the door-mat and been down to the pigpens and back up to Sven-son's house, and he doesn't exactly move with the speed of light. They must have discovered the body just about the time he arrived here, and after that there were police all over the place."

"I did wonder about the possibility of her having been transferred to another van and got out of town that way," said Helen, "but that doesn't seem likely because they've had all those roadblocks out for the men who held up the Carlovingian Crafters, and I can't imagine a police-man's not remembering a truck that had a great big pig in it. I expect they'd have given it a specially careful search, don't you? It would seem like such a good dodge, hiding the gold and silver in with Belinda."

"By George, it would, wouldn't it?" her husband agreed. "Barring the minor details that they'd somehow or other have to get the bullion and the pig together, that both take up a good deal of space so it would have to be something in the nature of a moving van to fit them in, and that the ruse would be so clever that it would stick out a mile that somebody was being clever, so the police would be down on them like hawks on a hen. Anyway, the robbery took place about twenty-five miles from here, and we have no reason to suppose that the one had anything to do with the other. If those two thieves had ever had any dealings with the college, I'd have recognized them, or somebody would have, considering the careful descriptions we were able to give. If they hadn't, how in Sam Hill would they know how to go about putting the snatch on Belinda?"

"Maybe they disguised themselves."

"In what? False beards? Speaking of beards, how about that face fungus of Frank Flackley's? Yea or nay? Iduna, he was sticking closer to you than bubble gum to a shoe sole last night: What do you think?"

"It's real," said their guest. "Don't ask me what he's wearing it for, unless maybe to save himself the price of a face-lift like my Uncle Elmer, who was vain as a peacock, cheap as dirt, and homely as a mud fence underneath, or so they claimed. I never saw him without his beard, myself. He used to put it up in kidskin curlers every night of his life. Anyhow, I'd be willing to bet my Sunday corset Mr. Flackley didn't grow that bush overnight."

"Too bad," sighed Helen. "I had a beautiful vision of ripping it off his face and shrieking, 'Thou art the man!' like the heroine of a Victorian novel. Peter, were you planning to talk with Thorkjeld this morning?"

"If I can find him," Shandy replied. "He'll probably rip my face off because I haven't hauled off a miracle and got this mess straightened out."

"Before he does," his wife reminded him gently, "do you think you might have a chance to do something about Birgit?"

Shandy groaned. "What, for instance?"

"Dearest, how do I know? Perhaps you could talk to Sieglinde. Sound her out."

"I thought you were going to do that."

"Very well, my love, if you don't feel up to it. Shall I come with you?"

"No, that might look too obvious. You know what it's like trying to get anything past that pair. I'll dree my own weird. You keep the home fires burning."

Shandy put on his veteran mackinaw and started up toward Valhalla, where the President reigned in a handsome white house of the Greek Revival period, as a New England college president should. He was hoping Birgit herself would open the door so he could get in a little sounding-out at the source of the difficulty, but it was Sieglinde, the President's lady, who flung wide the portal.

"Come in, Peter," she said. "Do you bring good news?"

"That depends on what you mean by good news," he hedged.

"Any news would be better news than we've been having," she sighed.

Now that Shandy had quit committing outrages against public propriety and settled down in lawful wedlock with a woman of whom she thoroughly approved, Sieglinde had mellowed a great deal in her manner toward him. In fact, the Shandys and the Svensons were as close to being intimate personal friends as the delicate diplomatic balance within a close-knit academic community allowed.

"Well," he began, "the good news is that Harry Goulson wants to give Miss Flackley a bang-up funeral on the house, for auld lang syne."

"I am pleased to hear that. It has been a source of concern to me how the obsequies would be handled. All must be done, however, with dignity and grace."

"I think you can rest easy on that point. Goulson plans to give her exactly the same kind of funeral as her father before her had. He even wants to use the old horse-drawn hearse in which the Goulsons have hauled the Flackleys to the family plot since God knows when."

"How sensitive and understanding of him! That is what she herself would have chosen, no doubt. Miss Flackley must have had great respect for family tradition, else why would she have carried on her father's business as she did? So also does Harry Goulson. I have always felt he is not sufficiently honored in the community. Please tell him the college chapel is available if he wishes, although he may well be planning to hold the service at the village church, where the previous funerals have been."

"Well—er—I expect Goulson's already arranging that part," said Shandy, "but what he does want from the college is the loan of two horses to draw the hearse."

"Two horses? Two of our Balaclava Blacks?"

The serenity of Sieglinde's exquisite countenance was marred for a fleeting second. "I do not know what Thorkjeld will say to that. I expect it will be something loud and profane."

"Goulson did mention something about borrowing a pair from somebody in Hoddersville or Lumpkin Corners if the President would prefer," Shandy interjected slyly.

"Impossible! Ah, now I know what Thorkjeld will say." Sieglinde's face was serene again. "You must tell him exactly that, and all will go as Mr. Goulson wishes. Only you must be careful not to ask for Odin or Thor."

"Helen mentioned Loki. She's got it into her head that Miss Flackley was especially fond of Loki, for some reason."

"If Helen thinks so, she is right. Helen is a woman of great wisdom. Besides, a funeral will exactly suit Loki's melancholy temperament. Ask for Loki and Tyr. Tyr is nearest in size. Also Tyr is lazy and it will do him good to work a little extra. He is not entered for the plowing contest."

Here was the opening Shandy had been praying for. "That's right, young Olafssen is working with Hoenir and Heimdallr, isn't he? How's he making out? Birgit feeding him up on lots of wheat germ and carrot juice?"

For the second time in the space of two minutes, and this was highly unusual, Sieglinde evinced perturbation.

"I do not know what Birgit is doing with Hjalmar. Peter, Thorkjeld and I are troubled in mind."

She drew out a chair and motioned him to sit. "I tell you this because you are a friend, because you are a man of discernment, and because if I do not tell somebody I shall blow my stack."

His heart in his mouth, he asked the unavoidable question. "What seems to be the matter?"

"That is our problem, Peter, we do not know! We have discussed and agreed, we should like Hjalmar for a son-in-law. When Birgit started bringing that boy home for dinner, I did not even mind making soybean cutlets. Hjalmar is not only handsome and brilliant when he is not being stupid, he is good, Peter! He is good as Thorkjeld is good, only of course less handsome and less intelligent, and sometimes a little bit dull in comparison to my husband."

"You find Olafssen dull?" Shandy asked in a somewhat stupefied tone.

"Compared to my husband I find anybody dull," she replied fondly. "In any case, that would not matter because Birgit has temperament enough for two. For several. She will be a good farmer's wife because there will be so much to do that she will have to stay out of agitations and never be bored, and he will be a great farmer because he has the calling. Hjalmar is poor, but we are not, and there is always the Endowment Fund."

One of the many things that made Balaclava Agricultural College unique was its policies with regard to financial assistance for students. During their years at the school, students got nothing for nothing. Loans and scholarships were not handed out on a platter. Jobs, on the other hand, were plentiful. Any student who needed to earn his way through was given the opportunity; anybody who had the opportunity and didn't make the most of it was dropped.

The rationale was simple: farmers were going to have to work hard all their lives anyway. If they couldn't hack it when they were young and strong, why encourage them to hope they'd be able to manage later?

Once a student was graduated, however, the situation changed. Cash was handed out generously to those who could show need, merit, and concrete proposals for making the most of what was given. Through these grants, many farms and small family businesses had been rescued from the developers and the conglomerates. Balaclava students could face the future with confidence, knowing the school would make sure they had a future to face.

The money was always in the form of an outright gift. However, it was understood that as the ex-student throve and prospered, he or she would return what had been taken from the Endowment Fund. Few had ever failed to do so; many had returned it threefold and more. There was plenty of cash on hand, there was no earthly reason why a chap like Hjalmar would not qualify for a grant, and there'd be no false qualms about nepotism if the Svensons couldn't get him and Birgit settled without one. Shandy still had no inkling as to why Sieglinde was so upset.

"Then what's the problem?" he repeated.

"Peter, you are dense today. Already, I have told you I do not know. Birgit will not say, she only shuts herself in her room and cries. That is not my Birgit. To yell, to stamp her feet, to throw things, to organize a mob and start a riot, all this is normal behavior and I know how to handle it, but to mope around with a white face and red eyes like the Easter bunny and not eat so much as one alfalfa sprout, what am I to do?"

"You don't suppose by any chance she's—er—"

"Been up to some hanky-panky and got herself pregnant?" Sieglinde finished for him. "Naturally, I thought that. It is the first thing any mother would think. But what great tragedy if she did? She knows I would not approve of her setting a bad example to the other young women in the college, but she knows also that her father and I would support her and Hjalmar in their picklement. We would give a little wedding, no fanfare of trumpets and beating of drums but nice with flowers, here in our own parlor with family and perhaps you and Helen and a few old friends, and a smorgasbord after. Then she and Hjalmar would finish school and we would do what we would do anyway, only sooner than expected. It is not that. Believe me, Peter, I should know. I have had seven of my own. Anyway, Birgit says not and Birgit does not lie. If she cannot tell the truth she says nothing. Seldom has she ever said nothing, except not to snitch on her sisters. Among the sisters is great love, but even to them she says nothing."

"Have you asked Hjalmar? Perhaps it's just a lovers' quarrel or something of that sort."

"There has been no quarrel. I have asked Hjalmar, and he says he does not know. He says he loves Birgit and has no wish to quarrel. Then I wonder if Birgit has perhaps changed her mind about Hjalmar, but she cries even harder and says no, she still loves him, and, Peter, I believe both."

"Does young Olafssen seem—er—concerned about the situation?"

"Concerned is not the word! He is frantic. He says to me, 'Mrs. Svenson, what the heck is wrong with her? Why won't she talk to me?' And all I can say to him is why won't she talk to her father, why won't she talk to her sisters, why won't she talk to her own mother? I tell you frankly, Peter, today Hjalmar is in no condition to plow a straight furrow two feet long, much less win the Juniors' competition. And Thorkjeld has worked so hard with him! He has shown such great promise. Last week we were all joking about drinking toasts at Birgit's wedding from the two cups our noble plowmen were going to win, and now this!"

Incredibly, Sieglinde Svenson, the Admirable Snowlady, broke down. "And Miss Flackley murdered in the college pigpens and our adorable Belinda of Balaclava missing and our beloved Professor Stott facing the ruin of thirty years' work and the Competition only a few days away and not even anybody left to shoe the horses!"

"Oh, come," said Shandy. "It's not quite that bad. The horses have already been shod, and anyway, we do have a new farrier. Didn't your husband tell you that another Flackley's taking over? His name is Frank and he's a nephew of the—er—former incumbent."

"As Birgit would say, if she would say anything," sniffed Mrs. Svenson, "big deal! How do we know if he can even choose which side of a horseshoe is up? Peter, do you realize all these terrible things have happened since those horseshoes on the stable doors were turned upside down? Your dear Helen kidnapped by those horrible robbers, Belinda gone, Miss Flackley gone, my Birgit changed from a proud young lioness to a weeping little mousess. Oh, where will it end?"

"It will end with our getting Belinda back and Olafssen's winning the Juniors' cup and all of us getting stuffed to the eyeballs with herring at Birgit's wedding," said Shandy with a good deal more conviction than he felt. "Cheer up, Sieglinde. Helen came out of the kidnapping unharmed, and I don't mind telling you I was a damn sight more worried about her than you are about Birgit. By this time next week, we'll all be wondering what we were so het up about."

"By this time next week, we shall also have buried Miss Flackley," the President's wife reminded him. "Do not try to play word games with me, Peter Shandy. Only please, please find out why my Birgit will not talk to me!"

Chapter 12

As Shandy was standing there wondering if he should go away or try to comfort the woman, President Svenson himself came down the stairs. Sieglinde at once dried her eyes.

"Well, Thorkjeld?"

"She won't talk to me, either," he growled. "What the hell do you want, Shandy?"

"Loki and Tyr."

It wasn't what he'd meant to say, but at this juncture it would probably do as well as anything else. At least it jolted Svenson out of his despondency.

"Hah?"

"Harry Goulson wants to borrow Loki and Tyr to draw the hearse for Miss Flackley's funeral," Shandy explained. "He's giving her an old-time send-off like her father before her."

"What the hell for?"

"Because she deserves it."

"Ungh."

"Does that mean yes?"

"Oh, what the hell do I care? Take the whole damn team," Svenson roared. "Shandy, what would you do if your daughter bawled all the time and wouldn't tell you why?"

"To the best of my knowledge, I don't have a daughter."

"Well, Yesus, man, you have an imagination, haven't you? Make believe you have a daughter."

"It's a bit difficult," Shandy began cautiously, "but—and, mind you, this is only theory based on inexperience—I think I'd act as if nothing were the matter. Maybe Birgit's just—er—going through a period of rebellion. Perfectly normal in young persons of that age."

"She's been rebelling since the day she was born. Came out head first yelling at the doctor and hasn't shut up since."

"Then perhaps the only way Birgit can rebel is to—er—not."

"That the best you can do?"

It was certainly not the worst he could do, though he'd hardly dare say so to these unhappy parents. Birgit's odd behavior could hardly be taken as proof that she'd had anything to do with those twenty-six sunflower seeds in Miss Flackley's van, but if she weren't sick or pregnant or on the outs with her boyfriend, what else could it mean?

"Er—I wonder if perhaps the best plan mightn't be to wait a bit and see what develops?" he temporized. "How long has she been this way?"

"Since yesterday morning," said Sieglinde.

Shandy groaned inwardly. Outwardly, he put on a show of relief.

"Oh, then that explains it, don't you think?"

"No," said Svenson.

"But it should be—er—obvious enough, shouldn't it? Birgit has taken a militant stand against Professor Stott's pig-breeding project. Now Stott's in serious trouble and she is—er—overcome with remorse at her—er—hostile behavior."

Sieglinde gave her eyes a final wipe and brightened a little. "Now, Peter, you begin to make sense. It is true that Birgit has been giving our dear Professor Stott a hard time. It is also true that she loves him since a baby, as who could not? I cannot think that Birgit herself would be a party to the kidnapping of Belinda. However, she may believe that her words have inspired others to commit this action and that she is thus guilty by association. If so, it is a terrible lesson but one she has to learn by herself. Peter says wait. I think we wait. Go now, Thorkjeld, and telephone Mr. Goulson about the horses."

"What horses?"

"Loki and Tyr, whom you have promised to lend so they can draw the hearse for Miss Flackley's funeral."

"The hell I have! Is he out of his mind, wanting our horses during the Competition?"

"I told him he couldn't have the funeral then, and he said he knew better than to think of it," Shandy said. "He did mention that if it's not convenient for the college to lend him a pair of Blacks, he could ask some of the boys from Hoddersville or Lumpkin Corners."

"Never! What's the number, Sieglinde? I'll straighten that bird out in a hurry. Never mind, I'll go down there in person. Hoddersville hacks! Urgh!"

Svenson went thundering off. His wife nodded with satisfaction to Shandy.

"That is good. It will relieve him to yell at somebody, and Mr. Goulson will not care because he will get the horses. Thank you, Peter. Now please go and find out why Birgit is crying."

"Do you mean you want me to go up and talk to her?"

"Of course not. She would not even let you in. Find out who has killed Miss Flackley and stolen our Belinda, then she will at least know if she has something to cry about. It is entirely possible, indeed I think more than probable, that she does not. However, it has never yet occurred to Birgit that she might be wrong about something, so you will need to bring proof."

"What sort of proof?"

"You will know when you find it. Go, Peter. I ask you as a friend and as a mother."

Shandy went. Reason told him that he was probably leaving the solution behind him as he turned his back on Valhalla, but it was some comfort that Sieglinde has been so emphatic about Birgit's not being personally involved in Belinda's disappearance and its terrible corollary. She might be a doting mother, but she was also a sensible, intuitive woman. By now she must know a remarkable lot about young people in general and daughters in particular.

But she didn't know about those twenty-six sunflower seeds in the van. Shandy heaved a mighty sigh, wondering where to start on this distasteful quest. He supposed he might as well go hunt up young Olafssen, for whatever that might be worth, though finding him could be a problem in itself. Olafssen being who he was, the odds were about equal that the senior student was either performing some doughty feat of heroism on the topmost peak of Old Bareface or falling into the soggiest mudhole in some swamp or other.

Stott might be able to help. Recalling what Helen had mentioned about squadrons and geodetic survey maps, Shandy perked up a trifle. If anybody could predict the whereabouts of that human lightning bolt, it should be Stott. Now the problem was to find Stott, and the answer to that one might very well lie in his own kitchen. He brightened one more degree and turned his steps briskly homeward.

He didn't get as far as the kitchen. A police cruiser was standing out in the Crescent and a young officer was right behind Helen when she came to the door.

"Oh, Peter, I'm so glad you're back. I just called the Svensons', hoping to catch you there. Sergeant Lubbock, here, wants us to go with him."

"What for?" Shandy demanded. "Not another—"

"No, Professor, nothing like that," the young man assured him. "The thing is, we've located a van we think might have been used in that robbery out at the Carlovingian Crafters. We're hoping you might be able to identify it."

"I already did. While I was waiting for my wife to turn up, I gave your people a complete description of the infernal thing, down to the smallest wrinkle in the blasted carpet. I saw enough of the dratted vehicle while I was cramming it full of bullion."

"Yes, sir, but, you see, the van's been torched."

"If you mean set fire to, why don't you say so?" said Shandy testily. "All right, I suppose we'll have to go take a look. Got your coat, Helen? How long is this going to take, Sergeant? We happen to be rather busy around here just now."

"I know, sir. As a matter of fact, it was a member of one of your search parties who found the van. It's approximately twelve miles from here, in a wooded area not far from the main highway that leads to the Crafters. Your student was equipped with a walkie-talkie—I mean a portable radio transmitting device—and used it to summon police assistance. I happened to be cruising in the area and responded to the call."

A pleasantly reminiscent expression crept over the

young trooper's attractive face. "Miss Gables led me down into the ravine where she'd discovered the wrecked vehicle. Cutest little bottom—er—that is, the van was at the bottom of the ravine. After having examined the evidence, I returned to my cruiser and made radio contact with headquarters. I was then instructed to request your aid in attempting an identification. Miss Gables promised to remain on guard, and I'd sure like to—that is, it is my official duty to relieve her as quickly as possible. Er—you don't happen to know her first name, do you? For my report, that is."

"It's Matilda," Helen told him as she pulled on her gloves and picked up her handbag.

"Matilda, eh?"

The sergeant rolled the syllables around his tongue, enjoying their flavor. "That's sort of nice. Different, you might say. I bet her boyfriend calls her Tilly."

Helen caught the wistful note of inquiry in his voice and replied kindly, "I don't believe she has one at the moment. Our nice farm boys aren't quite her style. Ready, Peter? We mustn't leave Miss Gables there alone too long."

"Gee, no," said Sergeant Lubbock.

"I suppose there's always the chance of her being attacked by hostile chipmunks," said Shandy rather nastily. "Come on, then, let's get this over with."

Mirelle Feldster was, of course, goggling from behind her living room curtains as they got into the police car. Shandy had a mad impulse to ask Lubbock to handcuff them, but thought better of it. Mirelle could supply enough dramatic touches without visual aids.

Lorene McSpee was out scrubbing her employer's front doorsteps, but hardly bothered to look up at what was happening across the way. She only waved her scrub brush in a sort of backhand salute, then went back with her unlikely task.

"That woman must be nutty as a fruitcake," Shandy remarked. "Doesn't she know by now that in about ten minutes Tim will come back from taking soil samples somewhere, caked to the eyebrows with mud?"

"She makes him go around to the back and take off his boots before he enters the house," said Helen. "Mary Enderble told me."

"Good God! Is there no end to her perfidy? We'd better phone Jemmy and tell her to shoot along another batch of baby pictures, quick."

"Peter dear, I do wish you wouldn't pin your hopes too high. It's my unfortunate duty to inform you that Frank Flackley happened to drop in again this morning, on his way to Hoddersville."

"But Hoddersville's in the opposite direction."

"Exactly," said his wife. "Please don't glare at me like that. It's not my fault. It's not Iduna's, either. She simply draws them, like moths to a flame."

"Would you happen to be talking about that pretty blonde lady who offered me a doughnut?" asked Sergeant Lubbock.

Shandy groaned. "Not you, too?"

"Not me, Professor. On my salary I couldn't even feed a woman that size. I thought I'd find a cute little one and work up gradually."

"Work up to what?"

"To getting married, I guess. I don't go much for this no-strings jazz. I see too much of what happens when people try to duck responsibility."

Shandy nodded. "Well spoken, young man. You'd have done well at Balaclava. Ever thought of becoming a farmer?"

"No, sir, I never wanted to be anything but a cop. Even when I got the scholarship—"

"What scholarship was this?" Helen prodded gently.

The sergeant blushed. "To Dartmouth."

"I was still too young for the police academy, so I figured I might as well take it. By the time I got my bachelor of science degree, I was almost twenty, so I pestered the police academy for a while, and finally they let me in on account of my making Phi Beta Kappa and whatnot."

"And now you're driving a state police cruiser."

"Yes, ma'am," said Sergeant Lubbock, grinning from ear to ear. "I made the grade at last. And now I'm afraid we're about as close to the van as we can get with the cruiser. Think you folks can manage a little climb?"

Chapter 13

Helen had sensibly put on boots and heavy slacks; Peter was already dressed for scrambling down wooded slopes. They were able to show Sergeant Lubbock, at least to their own satisfaction, that he didn't have a pair of doddering ancients on his hands.

They did have a bit of trouble convincing themselves that the mass of blackened, twisted metal at the bottom of the ravine had in fact been a van. Matilda Gables had been true to her trust. She was standing guard over the wreckage, looking peaked and woebegone, as if she'd been overtaxing her strength. However, she did manage a wan smile when she saw them coming toward her.

"What's the matter? Think we weren't coming back?" Sergeant Lubbock's smile was dazzling in its warmth. He really was a decorative note on the landscape, with his somehow still spic-and-span uniform, and not even a dollop of mud on his boots.

"Here, Miss Gables," he said, taking the tiny scholar by the arm and escorting her tenderly to a moss-covered rock, "you'd better sit down and rest a minute. Let me hold that walkie-talkie for you. Miss Gables has been doing a great job here, Professor Shandy. I guess you people all know each other."

"Oh yes." Helen went over and took Matilda's small, cold hand. "Matilda's one of my favorite borrowers at the college library. She never licks her fingers before she turns the pages."

"Bad habit, licking your fingers," said the state policeman affably. "That's how you leave clear fingerprints."

Helen was surprised to feel the young woman's hand jerk convulsively under her grasp.

"Matilda," she said, "I think this searching business has been too strenuous for you. You'd better ride back with us and get some rest. But first I suppose we might as well try to do what we came for. Heavens, this thing is a mess, isn't it? Peter, do you see anything that looks even vaguely like the van we were involved with?"

"Beyond the fact that it would probably be about the right size if we could straighten it out and that it seems to have been a Chevy, as the other was, I don't find much to go on," said her husband. "Is any trace of the paintwork visible?"

Matilda Gables shook her head. "I went over the wreckage inch by inch while I was waiting for you. I couldn't see a speck of color anywhere."

"That was good thinking, Miss Gables," said Lubbock. "Did you run across anything at all that looked interesting?"

"Only this."

She pointed to a scrap of metal that might once have been a door panel. "See those funny scratches? I think they must have been done deliberately. Doesn't that look like an M to you?"

Helen gasped. "Peter, it is! I must have done that myself while I was tied up and blindfolded. I was right up against the back door, praying the load wouldn't shift and squash me, and I could feel bare metal behind me. I got the notion of scratching my initials on it with the diamond in my ring. I don't know why; it was just to make myself feel a degree less helpless, I suppose. Don't you think that by a wild stretch of the imagination, those scratches look a little bit like H.M.S.? My maiden name was Helen Marsh," she explained to Lubbock.

"Oh yes," said Matilda Gables excitedly. "See where she tried to cross the H, and that squiggly one at the end could easily be an S. Besides, the scratches are quite fresh. I wiped the smoke off this little corner here, and it's not a bit rusty underneath."

"Say, what's a girl like you doing in a cow college?" Sergeant Lubbock was almost bursting with admiration by now. "Ever thought of the police academy?"

Miss Gables flushed. "They wouldn't have me. I'm too little."

"No, you're not. You're the perfect size. I mean, well, sure they have certain regulations in the uniformed branch because you have to be able to do all that police brutality stuff like picking up old ladies who've been knocked down and mugged, and being run over by hopped-up kooks you're trying to keep from killing themselves on motorcycles. But there's lab work, lie detecting, fingerprint analysis, photography, toxicology, lots of real fun jobs. You'd be a whiz!"

"I don't believe I ever fully appreciated the scope of police work before," Miss Gables replied, her face losing some of its lost-kitten expression. "I've always thought of you people more as repressive tools of a property-oriented society."

"Yeah, we do a little repressing now and then. But remember one thing, Miss Gables: the Force is always with us!"

She giggled. Shandy cleared his throat.

"Sergeant Lubbock, you have a—er—public duty to give Miss Gables further enlightenment on this interesting subject. However, I'm wondering if it might be done —er—for instance, over a cup of coffee at the Student Union? Mrs. Shandy and I have some rather urgent business back home. Miss Gables, can you manage to contact Professor Stott on that gadget and explain that you're leaving the search party to—er—cooperate with Sergeant Lubbock?"

"Professor Stott isn't my squadron leader," said Miss Gables primly.

"Then who is?"

A flush began at the point of the tiny chin and spread to the roots of the soft light-brown hair. She spoke a name in hushed reverence.

"Hjalmar Olafssen."

Sergeant Lubbock made a noise that might best be described as a snort.

"Oh, Jesus, that klutz! Sorry, Professor Shandy, that was undepartmental language, and feel free to report me if you so desire. I'll bet you a nickel cash money, though, that we get a rush call for a bulldozer to pull him out of the only patch of quicksand in Balaclava County. Did you happen to be at the sheep trials two years ago, when he fell over the collie? I laughed so much I had to go home and get my mother to sew up my uniform seams."

"I don't find that the least bit amusing," said Miss Gables huffily.

"Were you there?"

"No," she admitted. "I wasn't in college then."

"Oh. Too bad. We could have shared a beautiful memory. Of course I did think for a second or two that he was going to be mobbed and scalped by your entire student body. I was trying to remember what it says in the police manual about riot control when he sat up with that klutzy grin on his face and started apologizing to the dog. I guess Olafssen's a sort of natural-born clown, eh? Okay, Miss Gables, let's see if we can reach him, and explain carefully in words of one syllable that you're leaving the area."

Seeing that the young woman was in real distress over this tearing down of her idol, Shandy remarked, "I shouldn't care to have you get a false impression of the —er—mental caliber of Balaclava students, Sergeant Lubbock. Olafssen can and does show a high degree of intelligence at times. That—er—happened not to be one of the times."

This apparently happened to be another. They made contact easily enough, but they couldn't seem to make the squadron leader understand who Matilda Gables was. At last Olafssen was persuaded to consult the list Professor Stott had given him, find her name, and cross it off. The state police sergeant shook his head.

"You're trying to tell me that guy has all his marbles and he can't remember a dish—I mean a young lady like Miss Gables?"

"We—er—have a fairly large student body," Shandy replied. "As a senior, Olafssen doesn't have a great deal of contact with underclass—er—persons. He—er—no doubt knows her by sight if not by name."

"If he doesn't, he must be blind as well as dumb," said Lubbock as he shepherded the midget sophomore up the bank, keeping, as Shandy noted with some amusement, slightly to the rear in order to enjoy the view.

It was as well he did. From the front, Miss Gables presented a less charming picture. Her face was scarlet and her hazel eyes behind their absurd barn-owl spectacles were blurred with tears. Shandy felt mildly sorry for the child, but was content to let Lubbock cheer her up. The young sergeant was obviously having a red-letter day, between Helen's identification of the van and Miss Gables's form-fitting jeans. Lubbock's jubilation began to get on Shandy's nerves.

"I must confess," he said crossly, "I can't see how this burned out van is going to be much help in rounding up those crooks."

"We'll get'em," said Lubbock. "We've sent out those Identikit sketches made from your description to all stations. We're keeping up the roadblocks, and there's just no way those guys are going to get through with a load like the one they're toting."

"Still, you have no tangible evidence as to where they might be?"

"No, sir," Lubbock admitted. "They seem to have dropped out of sight. But at least we know now that they've shifted the loot to a hiding place or some other vehicle. That's a step in the right direction, isn't it?"

"I suppose so."

The professor was surprised to realize how depressed he was. Those awkwardly scratched initials were too poignant a reminder of the danger Helen had been in, the agony he'd endured before she turned up safe, and of the pleasant woman who'd been murdered so soon after the only time she'd got to use the silverware they'd bought in her honor.

He clearly remembered helping Miss Flackley on with that brown mohair stole. It had felt thick and light in his hands, and he'd been glad the frail-looking woman had such a warm covering against the chill of the night.

Thinking of mohair reminded him of goats, which led to sheep and his intention to buttonhole young Olafssen on the subject of Birgit Svenson's sulking fit. Why hadn't he used that child's walkie-talkie to find the senior and get it over with while they were back there in the woods?

Perhaps because some part of his brain was still functioning. He couldn't have let the others go with him, and if they'd left without him he might have been stuck for hours waiting to get a lift home. It didn't matter. He could catch Olafssen later, assuming there really wasn't any quicksand in Balaclava County. If there was, Hjalmar would surely find it. On the whole, "klutz" wasn't such a bad description.

Was Matilda Gables beginning to think so, too? The petite sophomore appeared to be responding positively, though timidly, to Sergeant Lubbock's sales pitch on the need for brilliant young women in the Force. At times she looked up at him with the dawning of a new interest. Once or twice she smiled as winsomely as any young man could expect. Helen sat watching the tableau with a benign smile twitching about her lips, and Shandy was able to derive some pleasure from seeing his wife thus entertained.

As they neared the college, however, Helen's expression grew vaguely troubled, then definitely perplexed. Things were not going right in the front seat; in fact, Matilda was beginning to cry. When they neared her dormitory, she begged to be let out and dashed off before Sergeant Lubbock could so much as request her phone number for official purposes.

A trooper to the bone, Lubbock endeavored to hide his chagrin, but he couldn't fool Helen. Leaning forward, she remarked ever so casually, "I'm afraid you struck a nerve with Matilda Gables, Sergeant. You're quite right about her not belonging at Balaclava, too; but it's going to be dreadfully hard for her to admit she's made such a stupendous mistake. Matilda's going to need a good deal of understanding and moral support. I'm afraid she may have a hard time finding it around this campus. Don't you agree, Peter?"

A well-directed kick on the ankle prompted Peter to agree that he did agree, even though every fiber of his loyal being rose up in protest against the suggestion that understanding and moral support were in short supply at Balaclava. It should, he thought be clear to the meanest intelligence that his wife was just trying to make this infatuated young squirt feel better, but Lubbock swallowed Mrs. Shandy's specious explanation hook, line, and sinker.

"Gosh, I'm sorry! I didn't mean to upset her. Do you think I ought to give her a buzz and apologize?"

"Why don't you wait a day or so, then give her a call —here, I'll write down the name of the dorm for you— and perhaps make a friendly suggestion that she join you somewhere for a chat and perhaps a bite to eat? I should warn you, though, that Matilda's a vegetarian, so you'd better make it a salad bar instead of a hamburger joint."

"Vegetarian, eh?" As he stopped in front of the brick house and moved to help Mrs. Shandy out, Lubbock's face broke into a grin. "So that explains it. I was wondering how those things got into the cruiser."

He nodded at the place where Matilda had been sitting. Scattered around the seat and floor were a number of sunflower seeds, perhaps twelve or fifteen. As a rule, either or both of the Shandys would have automatically picked them up and counted them. Right now, neither Peter nor Helen would have touched them with a ten-foot pole.

Chapter 14

Not even the warmth of Iduna's welcome could dispel the chill that was gripping the pair as they entered their house.

"Peter, it's just not possible," Helen protested. "That child could not have—"

"But all that crying and carrying on—"

"Don't you think that was only because Olafssen didn't—"

"With Lubbock ogling her buttocks?"

Iduna emitted a ladylike, "Hem! I hate to break up an interesting conversation, but President Svenson's waiting in the living room."

"It needed only that," said Shandy. "How long's he been here?"

"About an hour. We've been having a nice chat. He says I remind him of his wife's second cousin Ortrud."

"It's a good thing you don't remind him of his wife. We have enough shenanigans around here already."

He went to meet the inevitable. "Hello, President; to what do we owe the honor?"

"Urgh," said Svenson. "Where you been?"

"Identifying the van Helen got kidnapped in. One of our students found it. Matilda Gables, know her?"

That was a stupid question. President Svenson knew a great deal about every one of his students.

"Sophomore. Little smarty-pants with big glasses. One of Birgit's Viggies. Doesn't belong here. Vassar, Bryn Mawr, some highbrow place. Stuck on Olafssen, like the rest of'em. Wish the hell they wouldn't. Plenty of good guys going to waste. What the hell was she doing finding vans? She's supposed to be finding a pregnant sow, damn it! Too blasted intellectual to know the difference?"

"No, Miss Gables appeared to have a grasp on the—er—realities of the situation. It was just that the van—er—happened to be there."

"Urgh," said the President again, thus dismissing the student, the van, the entire subject. "Been to see Goulson. Got it set up. Tomorrow morning. Nine o'clock. Baptist church. Be there."

"Naturally," said Shandy. "Helen and I wouldn't dream of not attending. We liked Miss Flackley very much. Why so early?"

"Why not?" Svenson replied reasonably. "Get it over before word spreads and the vultures gather. Goulson's going to phone her old customers, neighbors, town fathers, people he thinks ought to pay their respects."

Shandy started for the door. "I'd better tell Helen right now. She'll want to order flowers."

"Siddown. All ordered. One from my wife and me, one from the animal husbandry department, one from you, one from Stott. Goulson's going to pick'em out and send you the bill."

"That's nice," Shandy grunted. "Have you informed Frank Flackley yet?"

"Ungh. Stopped in here a while back on the way from Hoddersville to Lumpkin Corners, for some damned reason. Twelve-mile detour. Man must be demented."

"Er—not necessarily. All roads seem to lead to Miss Bjorklund these days."

"Yesus, you got one, too? See why. Nice woman. Good-natured. Good pie. Good coffee. Good doughnuts. Keep her around."

"We're hoping to," said Shandy. "I've been thinking that perhaps she and Tim Ames—"

Svenson burst into guffaws. "The mountain and the squirrel!"

"Jemima was a big woman," said Shandy defensively.

"Not that big. Forget it, Shandy. You're barking up the wrong shins."

"But, drat it, President—"

Svenson wasn't interested in Shandy's protest. Having accomplished his mission, he heaved his great bulk out of the special chair Helen had bought to accommodate guests the size of him and Professor Stott and charged for the door.

"What was that all about?" Helen asked when Shandy went to find her, and perhaps a cup of coffee, in the kitchen.

"Miss Flackley's funeral. It's all set for nine o'clock tomorrow morning. The President has graciously ordered flowers to be sent in Stott's and our names. We get the bills, of course."

"How sweet of him!" Helen snapped. "Mightn't it have occurred to the man that we'd prefer to choose our own?"

"Of course not. I shouldn't be too disturbed, my love. Goulson's been appointed to make the choices, so I expect they'll be more or less appropriate. Call him if you want to."

"No, I don't suppose it makes any difference, really. It's not as though she had sisters and cousins and aunts who'd notice and care. I do think it's odd that such a charming woman wound up leading such a solitary life."

"If we're to believe Frank Flackley's theory—"

"Damn Frank Flackley!"

Helen almost never swore, thus the expletive emerged with special force from her lips. "Peter, you don't for one single moment credit the notion of her cuddling with Harry Goulson among the coffins?"

"Not Goulson, no. She might have had somebody somewhere, though. I hope she did."

"So do I."

"Er—speaking of hidden yearnings, you wouldn't happen to have a stray piece of that custard pie left over from last night's dinner?"

" 'Fraid not," said Iduna, who was manicuring potatoes at the sink. "That nice Mr. Svenson polished it off clean as a whistle. I thought for a second there he was going to lick the plate. He looked so downhearted when I had to apologize for not having any more to offer him. I thought I hadn't better say anything about the chocolate cream one I made today or we wouldn't have any left for our suppers. Could I interest you in a sliver of that now?"

"I think you just possibly might," said Shandy. "Will you ladies join me?"

"Too close to dinner for me," said Helen. "I'll have a cup of tea, though, to keep you company. No, please,

Iduna, I'll make it. Here, sit down and make believe you're a guest for a change."

Iduna pulled out a chair, albeit reluctantly. "No pie for me, thanks. I'll just settle for one or two of those oatmeal cookies in the jar. How'd you make out with that nice young policeman?"

"We think it's the same van. They'd run it over a banking and set fire to the wreck, so there wasn't much to go by, but I'd tried to scratch my initials in the metal with my diamond ring, and we did find some hen scratches that looked like them."

"There, now," said Iduna admiringly, "who but you would think of doing a brainy thing like that? I hope you didn't hurt that lovely ring any."

"Not that I can see. Peter always buys top quality."

Helen leaned over and kissed her husband on the cheek. "Don't you, dear?"

"It pays in the long run."

. With his mouth full of pie and his heart full of gratitude that Helen was here beside him instead of back there in that burned-out van, Shandy was beginning to feel better. He reached for the hand that wore his ring and held it close while he finished his snack.

"That pie is sheer poetry, Iduna. What else is on the menu for tonight?"

"I thought I'd better roast that chicken we bought yesterday before it starts to spoil. Can't trust a chicken too far, you know."

"How well I know," said Shandy.

He thought of the evil-minded hens he'd been forced to feed as a child back on the home farm. Then he thought of those two weepy chicks, Birgit Svenson and Matilda Gables. Matilda was one of Birgit's Vigilant Vegetarians, and there was that damnable, irrefutable fact of the sunflower seeds scattered around Sergeant Lubbock's cruiser exactly as they had been in Martha Flackley's farriery van.

They in turn led him to think of Hjalmar Olafssen. He'd have to trek over to Olafssen's dormitory after dinner. Perhaps he should call the Svensons first and make sure the love-sick swain wasn't up there languishing outside Birgit's bedroom window, or whatever. Perhaps he should sit here quietly for a while and have a look at the evening paper.

Half an hour later as he was nursing a preprandial Balaclava Boomerang, listening to Helen's and Iduna's seemingly inexhaustible flow of reminiscence about South Dakota, and realizing how tired he was, the problem of Olafssen solved itself. The handsome Junior Plowman, covered with leafmold, last year's burdocks, and other evidences of a day in the wilds, showed up on his own hook.

"Sorry to butt in on you like this, Professor."

"Not at all," said Shandy. "As a matter of fact, I was just wondering how to get in touch with you. I understand you came here to see me yesterday while I was out."

"Well, yeah."

Olafssen tripped over a footstool, set a floor lamp rocking like a kerosene lantern in the hand of a moonshiner who'd been consumer-testing his own product, got his feet snarled in a hooked rug depicting a scene from *The Peaceable Kingdom* of Edward Hicks, worked by Helen's Great-Aunt Marguerite, but somehow managed to fetch up in the armchair not long ago vacated by the man who might or, as the situation now stood, might not become his father-in-law.

"Oh, that miserable rug," said Helen, tactfully rescuing her treasured family heirloom. "It's always getting in somebody's way. Could we offer you a Boomerang, Olafssen?"

Her suggestion was in accordance with faculty etiquette. Freshmen were served such beverages as sweet cider, hot chocolate with marshmallows, or iced lemonade, as the season dictated. Sophomores were gravely asked if they preferred tea or coffee. Juniors might be invited to partake of beer or a light wine. Seniors could have whatever the host cared to serve.

Thus a pattern was set for the entire college. Since the upper-class members were jealous of their prerogatives, any tendency to intemperance among the lowlier ranks was quickly squashed. Nobody was forced by peer pressure to imbibe what he wasn't yet ready to handle, and what could be a serious problem in other institutions simply did not exist at Balaclava.

"A Boomerang would be fine," said Olafssen. "I could sure use a pick-me-up."

It was a stricken giant who sat dripping peat moss on The Peaceable Kingdom. The student looked as if he hadn't been sleeping. His face, which should have been given no more than a healthy glow by two days of scrambling among the foothills of Old Bareface, showed an exhaustion that could not be merely physical. Decidedly, Olafssen had something on his mind.

Shandy waited till his guest had gulped half a glassful of hard cider and cherry brandy in one mighty swallow and got his eyes back into their sockets and his breathing under control. Then he asked quietly, "What's the matter, Olafssen?"

"Gosh, I— Oh, heck! Since I came to tell you, I s'pose I might as well. It's about Miss Flackley's van."

The young man stared moodily at the remaining half of his Balaclava Boomerang until Shandy had to prompt him again.

"What about Miss Flackley's van?"

"Well—see—I was in it."

"Oh, Christ! When?"

"The night before she was killed, when she was having dinner with you folks. See, there was this talk at the auditorium."

"There often is."

"Well, this one was about peddling in the early days, so Birgit and I decided to take it in. We'd been reading *Yankee Peddlers.**

Again Olafssen lapsed into moody silence. Again Shandy had to prod him.

"Nothing incriminating in that, so far. I've read *Yankee Peddlers* myself. So has Mrs. Shandy."

"Well, sure, everybody has. I mean, you'd have to have rocks in your head not to, wouldn't you?"

"You'd miss a rewarding experience, certainly."

"Well, see, that was the problem. The book moved along fast, kept you interested, but this speaker didn't. He was showing a bunch of slides that were enough to put you to sleep, so Birgit and I sneaked out and—well, we thought we might as well find someplace where we could—"

"Sit down and compare notes on the lecture?"

"Yeah, that's right. Well, see, there weren't hardly any

---

* It is assumed that Olafssen was referring to *The Yankee Peddlers of Early America,* by J. R. Dolan. Dr. Porble reports that the library's copy has been sent out for rebinding.

cars in the lot. Most people walked down, I guess. But Flackley the Farrier's van was sitting there—"

"Unlocked?"

"Well, sure. Nobody bothers much about locking cars around here, except during the Illumination. You know that. Anyway, we figured she wouldn't mind if we sat in it for a while. So anyway, we—well, we sat in it for a while."

"And then what?"

Olafssen shrugged. "Then when we figured it was about time for the guy to turn the lights back on, we sneaked back into the hall."

"And that was all?"

"That was all. Only Birgit hasn't spoken to me since."

"Would you care to tell me what went on in the van?"

"Well, heck, nothing out of the ordinary."

"The ordinary being what?"

The young man blushed. "Well, heck, I mean, weren't you ever alone in a parked car with a girl you were crazy about?"

"Wasn't he ever?" Helen murmured.

Shandy ignored her. "You didn't—er—attempt any undue liberties?"

"Are you kidding? In the Home Arts parking lot? With the President's daughter? You think I want to get stomped to a bloody pulp? Anyway, I respect Birgit."

"So you parted on—er—respectful terms?"

Olafssen grinned through his blushes. "I guess you could call it that. Anyhow, I was all set to walk her home, but the speaker asked me to help carry stuff out to his car and I was feeling kind of a skunk for ducking out on him, so I didn't like to refuse. I asked Birgit if she'd mind waiting a minute, but Miss Wrenne and Miss Waggoner and a few others were walking back up to Valhalla, so she said she might as well go with them. But she was perfectly okay about it. I mean, she gave me a little peck on the cheek right in front of Miss Wrenne and told me not to bust a leg on the way back to my dorm."

"Cupid could hardly have expected more from Psyche," said Shandy. "Then what?"

"Then, foof! That's just it, Professor, not one darn thing. I try to call her and she won't come to the phone. I go up there and she hides in her room with the door locked. I yell through the keyhole and she doesn't even yell back."

"All this since night before last?"

"Yeah. I did see her at the assembly yesterday morning, but I was stuck up in back with a bunch of the guys and she was down front at the other end of the bleachers. I saw her looking around once, so I waved and yelled, 'Hey, Birgie, up here,' you know how you do, but I don't know if she heard me or what. She never looked in my direction again, and when we broke up I lost her in the crowd. I kept looking for Birgie in the cafeteria and everywhere, but she was nowhere in sight, so I figured she must have gone to change her clothes, or something."

"But she shouldn't have had to," Helen pointed out. "Since she lives at home, she must have got a special message about the meeting or she wouldn't have shown up at all. Birgit would surely have put on boots and a warm jacket to come down from Valhalla. You don't recall what she was wearing?"

"I do," said Shandy suddenly. "I remember seeing her run down the path among the last lot to arrive and crowd in on the front end of the bleachers, as Olafssen says. She had on a bright purple jacket with a hood, and I believe pants to match. At least I have a general impression of—er—allover purpleness. She reminded me of Portulaca Purple Passion, which I suppose is why the picture sticks in my mind."

"That would be her cross-country ski suit," said Helen, "warm, windproof, lightweight, and easy to get about in. A very sensible choice for pig-hunting. So we can infer that she came dressed and ready to go, but never went. I wonder what happened to change her mind."

"I'm wondering why neither she nor Olafssen mentioned having been there when President Svenson asked whether anybody could shed light on the events of the previous night," Shandy said.

Olafssen looked uncomfortable. "Well, you already knew the van had been parked in the Home Arts lot. All we did was sit in it from maybe half-past eight till a little before nine o'clock. Miss Flackley was still with you then, wasn't she?"

He glanced around half fearfully, as if he thought the shade of the demised farrier might be lurking in some corner of the living room.

"And, heck, you know the Svensons. They're the greatest people in the world, but they're—well, sort of heavy on proper conduct. Birgit's supposed to set an example, and all that jazz."

"And sneaking out on a visiting lecturer to canoodle in the farrier's van wouldn't constitute the right sort of example, is that what you're getting at?"

"Well, I had a feeling her folks wouldn't think so. Anyway, I didn't want to say anything to her father before I'd cleared it with Birgit, only I never got the chance. It didn't seem right not to tell somebody, though, and I thought you'd be the safest. I mean, you're sort of officially involved, but I figured I could trust you not to get Birgit in Dutch with her folks."

"Olafssen, are you sure that's all you wanted to tell me?"

"That's it, Professor. Thanks for listening. And thanks for the Boomerang, Mrs. Shandy."

Chapter 15

"Peter, do you think he was telling the truth?" said Helen as they sat down to roast stuffed chicken and baked squash.

"I'm ready to believe what he told was the truth," Shandy replied. "I'm wondering if he did in fact tell the whole truth. It made sense to come forward with that information about his little necking party with Birgit because no doubt at least one other couple had the same idea and looked in to see who'd beaten them to the van. I presume he went back to his dorm when he said he did, and that Birgit walked up to Valhalla with Shirley Wrenne and Pam Waggoner because it would be ridiculous to lie about something so easy to check him up on. The question is, did both of them stay put once they'd got where they went?"

"Well, if you want my opinion for what it's worth, I'd say he was telling the plain, unvarnished truth," Iduna put in. "He was blushing like a girl on her first date, and he wasn't trying to look you square in the eye. It's been my experience, and Lord knows I've had enough of it renting rooms to students back home, that a good liar looks you straight in the eye and doesn't bat an eyelash and a bad liar at least tries to look you in the eye and maybe turns kind of red in the face, but he didn't and he did, if you get what I'm driving at."

"M' yes," said Shandy. "That's a good point, Iduna. Anyway, it's hard to believe any chap who can plow a straight furrow and understand the esoteric subtleties of cucumber scab would stoop to falsehood. That leaves us with a rather nasty alternative, doesn't it?"

"Do you mean Birgit and that little Gables girl?" cried Helen. "Peter, they couldn't!"

131

"No, the pair of them couldn't pull it off alone, and Sieglinde maintains Birgit wouldn't do such a thing, so let's consider another hypothesis. We do know that the Gables kid is bright, unhappy, and not especially popular at Balaclava. Those are the ingredients of a potential troublemaker, right?"

"I suppose so," Helen sighed, "but—"

"But me no buts. Let's assume for the sake of argument that Miss Gables hatches up a clever plot, inspired by that kidnapping episode in which we ourselves were so damnably involved, to purloin Belinda as a protest thing for the Viggies. Naturally, she goes to Birgit with her idea, but Birgit refuses to countenance it. She doesn't want to hurt Professor Stott herself, and she doesn't want Hjalmar involved in something that could put him out of the Competition and get him expelled two months before graduation. Having, as she thinks, put an end to Matilda's plan, she dismisses it from her mind. Young Matilda is ticked off and decides to go ahead on her own hook. She manages to enlist the aid of at least one other Viggie, whom I picture as large, strong, doltish, and male. When she learns, perhaps by attending that same lecture, that Miss Flackley's van is unexpectedly available, she whips into action."

"How, for instance?"

"She lurks. As she sees Stott homeward wend his weary way and Miss Flackley turn out of the parking lot, she rushes out from wherever she's lurking and flags down the van."

"The confederate would have to do that. Matilda would be too small to see in the dark."

"I concede you the confederate. In any event, Miss Flackley is told in pretended agitation that one of the animals is sick up at the barns, and can she come right this minute? She goes, of course. Presumably she and the flagger ride up together. As she alights from the van, she's seized from behind and muffled in her own mohair stole to prevent outcry."

"All right, then what?"

"Miss Gables would have a second vehicle waiting up at the pigpens. Her plan would be to hustle Miss Flackley into conveyance number two and keep her prisoner while they loaded Belinda into the van and took her to a hiding place. They'd then join forces up on Old Bareface. Miss

Flackley would then be put back into her own van, perhaps loosely bound as you were, in a spot where she
wouldn't be able to raise an immediate hue and cry when
she worked herself loose. The conspirators would hightail it for the college, and by the time Miss Flackley got
to a phone, they'd be snug in their dorms."

"But she'd know who they were."

"Not necessarily. She never mingled with the student
body, except those who had occasion to frequent the
animal barns while she was working there. It was dark,
remember, and they'd have kept their jacket hoods or
scarves or whatever up around their faces. At least they'd
intend to, but being a bunch of silly young amateurs, they
might flub it. Let's deduce from the sunflower seeds
found on the seat that Matilda is driving the van. The
confederate, having locked Miss Flackley in the other car
with her hands tied, or whatever, loads the sow aboard
and away goes Matilda with Belinda. You follow me so
far?"

"I follow you. Oh, Peter, you do make it sound horribly plausible."

"It gets more horrible when the other person tries to
get into the car with Miss Flackley. Perhaps she's managed to get her hands loose or recovered from the whiff
of ether they've given her or—Well, anyway, they strug-
gle. Miss Flackley must have been a lot stronger than
she looked, considering her profession. Her opponent has
more of a scrap than he bargained for. Perhaps he's holding that sharp little knife of hers. He might have used it
to prick the pig in the rump and make her climb into the
van. I can't imagine Belinda's making that sort of effort
without considerable persuasion. Anyway, somehow or
other the knife gets into somebody's hand and Miss
Flackley's throat is cut."

"By accident, you mean?"

"Oh yes, I should think so. Deliberate murder would
be no part of Matilda's plan. However, Miss Flackley is
dead. Naturally, the person who killed her panics, stuffs
the body into the feeder and goes ahead with the original
plan because he doesn't know what else to do. When he
reaches the rendezvous, he either confesses to Matilda
or, more probably, pretends to be shutting Miss Flackley
inside the back of the van and hustles the girl off before
she has a chance to find out her plan's gone wrong."

"Peter, you could be right. So when her father called her to the assembly next morning Birgit would conclude that Matilda went ahead with the plan despite her veto, and come charging down with fire in her eye to straighten out the Viggies. When she heard about Miss Flackley's horrible death and realized she might have prevented it if she hadn't been so cocksure about being able to control her little band of serious thinkers, she went into a tailspin. I wonder whether Thorkjeld told Birgit about the murder or just said, 'Come and hunt the pig.' He won't remember and she won't tell you. Unless her mother happened to overhear. You might ask Sieglinde."

"Later, perhaps. What difference does it make? I could sit here spouting theories till your ears fell off and none of them would amount to a hill of beans unless I could come up with some tangible evidence. Please pass the cranberry sauce."

"Oh, Helen," said Iduna, "were you with me at that church supper when Reverend Spottswold handed the cranberry sauce to Mrs. Olson just as she took a sneezing fit and her store teeth fetched loose and bit a big chunk out of that emerald-green rooster feather boa Mrs. Pleyer had got herself gussied up in?"

As a change of subject, it was a wow. Either because she sensed her husband was fed up with doom and gloom or because she herself couldn't take any more, Helen began to fill in the details with hilarious effect. Soon all three were in near convulsions. By the time they'd sobered down enough to start thinking about dessert, Timothy Ames dropped over to get away, as he explained, from the smell of chlorine bleach for a while. They played four-handed cribbage and gorged on chocolate cream pie and passed a generally pleasanter evening than any of them had expected.

In the morning, however, was the funeral. While Iduna was still adjusting her hat and Helen hunting for her best black kid gloves, faculty members and student representatives in sober attire began filing down the Crescent on their way to the Baptist church.

The animal husbandry department appeared in force. Jim Feldster, as a senior member, evidently felt himself obligated to take a leading part in the affair. Mirelle, in spite of the catty remarks she'd been making about Miss

Flackley ever since the murder, trotted right along beside him, laying it on, in Iduna's apt phraseology, for all she was worth.

Lorene McSpee, who could never have had occasion to know Miss Flackey but didn't intend to miss the show, joined the profession herding Professor Ames. Tim was looking wretchedly respectable in a dazzling white shirt and sharply pressed trousers, although he clung to his ratty old jacket as a child to its security blanket. Shandy, fidgeting by the window and wondering what took two grown women so long to get their coats on, was relieved to see John and Mary Enderble, twin souls of kindness, come out and form a protective bodyguard around Tim. John did not appear to have his mouse along. Had they hired a sitter, or did the mouse no longer require such frequent feedings? Probably the latter, mice being precocious creatures.

Now the Svensons loomed into view, Sieglinde looking inexpressibly beautiful and noble and faintly sad, as became the occasion. She had on her familiar blue tweed coat, but a new beret of a pale flax color since Thorkjeld had found he could no longer endure the sight of her old blue one and had torn it to shreds with a wild cry of "Arrgh!" for reasons she fully understood as a welling up from the unplumbable depths of his adoration.

Birgit and her two younger sisters were with their parents. Shandy couldn't see much of Birgit's face because she'd turned up her coat collar, wore a felt hat with its brim pulled down over her face, and had on dark glasses. She looked like a young Greta Garbo, and was being about as sociable and forthcoming as the Swedish star would have been under similar circumstances.

Just as Helen and Iduna at last announced themselves ready to swell the throng, Professor Stott lumbered along. He was impeccably garbed in a dark gray overcoat and a deep brown suit. His jaunty green porkpie hat had been replaced by a sober homburg that matched the suit. Had his head borne hair, not a strand would have been out of place. Nevertheless, he managed to convey a general effect of dishevelment. When they fell into step with him, he hardly seemed to notice he had company until Iduna ventured a remark that Miss Flackley would have been pleased by such a turnout.

His mien became perhaps half a degree less somber.

"Perhaps it would indeed have been a source of gratification. One hopes so. As the poet hath expressed it, the heart bowed down by weight of woe to weakest hope will cling, to thought and impulse while they flow that can no comfort bring. For myself, I confess, I see no comfort. Please forgive this unmanly urge to share the aforementioned weight of woe."

"What are friends for?" said Iduna. "Anyhow, I reckon my shoulders are broad enough to hold an extra woe or two."

"Miss Bjorklund, you are a tower of strength. I am emboldened to term you the star that illumines my dark night of tribulation. That you are so gracious as to employ the word 'friend' is, however, a felicity of which I find myself at this juncture undeserving. Miss Flackley has given her life in a vain effort to save Belinda, while I —I have striven, Miss Bjorklund, truly striven with every fiber of my being, but—"

He choked, and had to pause for recovery. "At this moment, I am so totally overwhelmed by a sense of failure that your kindness turns to gall. I feel degraded, unworthy."

"Now, now," said Iduna, laying a hand on his arm, "you won't be helping Belinda any if you let yourself get down in the dumps like this. You've just got to do like Columbus, sail on, sail on, sail on and on. We had to learn that piece in school when I was ten. They made me recite it at assembly. Oh my, was I scared!"

Stott's backbone stiffened. His shoulders squared. His majestically porcine features settled into a more resolute mold.

"You have great wisdom as well as a great heart, Miss Bjorklund. Sail on, sail on, sail on and on. That must indeed be our watchword until this grievous wrong has been righted."

Shandy personally didn't think much of that watchword, the nearest water being Cat Creek, which was unnavigable except by toy sailboat. He had an excellent memory for verse as a rule and was sure he could dredge up a better one. However, the only line that came to mind was from *The Cremation of Sam McGee*.

"Then I made a hike, for I didn't like to hear him sizzle so," hardly struck the note he was looking for. He wisely decided to leave Stott to Iduna and concentrated on piloting his wife safely into the church.

This was no small feat. Harry Goulson had certainly kept his vow to do Martha Flackley proud. The old hearse was waiting at the side door, shined up and ready to go as advertised. Loki and Tyr were in double harness, Loki wearing that sad, contemplative expression so appropriate to the occasion, Tyr quietly asleep standing up. The pair were groomed as for a competition, but with black leather bosses replacing the usual brass on their harnesses and slightly moth-eaten but still impressive plumes of black ostrich feathers adorning their heads. They looked magnificent. As Shandy waited his turn to enter the sanctuary, he caught many an envious glance fixed on the team, and no wonder.

Ninety and a hundred years ago, such owners of pure-bred Belgians, Clydesdales, and Percherons might have been joking about "Buggins's Bastards." The earliest interbreeding efforts of Balaclava Buggins and his twenty-three students had produced some odd-looking specimens, but now a single Balaclava Black colt might fetch a sum that would make a Shire horse look like a Shetland pony.

Exactly what the Balaclava Black bloodlines were only those in the highest college echelons knew, and they were sworn by a mighty oath to utmost secrecy. The Flackleys might have known. From earliest days, Flackleys had shod and doctored these mighty steeds that combined the size and stamina of a heavy draft horse with the agility of a trotter. There wasn't a horseman present who wouldn't give his eyeteeth to own Loki and Tyr, and Shandy knew it.

Just about every one of Miss Flackley's customers must be here. He recognized many of them from previous competitions: lean little men with lined faces and straight, thin lips; handsome women with straight backs, strong arms, and weather-beaten complexions; jowly men with enormous bellies; people of all sizes and descriptions, old, young, middle-aged. There were teen-aged girls who weren't trying to hide their tears; teen-aged boys with silver belt buckles in the shape of galloping mustangs, trying to pretend they weren't scared because somebody they'd depended on to show up on schedule as surely as they'd depended on morning to break and night to fall was never going to come and shoe their beloved horses again.

Frank Flackley was taking on an awesome responsibility. Shandy found himself wondering uneasily if the man was up to it. At any rate, Martha's nephew was behaving today with all the punctilio Harry Goulson could have desired. He was dressed in a decent suit of dark blue and had been down to Mac the Barber's. His hair was shorter, his beard neatly trimmed. He looked alone, bereft, and handsome enough to provoke fresh outbursts of weeping among the more susceptible women in the congregation.

Shandy sneaked a peek to see if Iduna was weeping, too, but she wasn't. Sitting beside Professor Stott, she looked suitably grave but composed. In fact, she looked surprisingly like Sieglinde Svenson, though more dashingly dressed. South Dakota must be a sartorial step ahead of Massachusetts, or at any rate of Balaclava County.

The minister remembered Martha Flackley from Sunday school. He talked about what sort of girl she'd been then, how she'd picked berries to help herself through normal school, how she'd enjoyel her years as a teacher, and how she'd bravely and uncomplainingly taken up the torch of the Flackleys after her brothers were killed and her father died.

He said a good many things that people who thought they'd known Martha Flackley for thirty years and more were finding out now for the first time in their lives. There must be many more than Peter Shandy who were mentally kicking themselves for never having taken the trouble to know her better. When the minister had finished his eulogy, Harry Goulson and his son, both of them fine singers, stood up and sang, "Beautiful Isle of Somewhere" in close harmony. That was when the sniffling really began.

The cemetery was less than a mile outside the village. After six of Martha Flackley's oldest acquaintances—neighbors, classmates, and a chap who'd been her star pupil when she taught sixth grade out at the Forks—had borne the coffin out to the hearse, Loki and Tyr began their solemn march up Main Street. Harry Goulson handled the reins. He had his son up on the seat beside him because this was a day he wanted the boy to remember.

Many followed the hearse on foot. Those who'd

brought their cars from faraway places like the Seven Forks and Hoddersville offered rides to anybody who wanted one. Even that highfalutin crowd from Lumpkin Corners showed, as Mrs. Lomax later remarked to her cat, a streak of human decency she'd never thought they had in them.

Shandy managed to keep close to the Svensons, watching what he could see of Birgit's face. She seemed to be neither more nor less affected by the ceremony than her peers, and this puzzled him a good deal. At last he could tolerate his own bewilderment no longer.

"Helen," he murmured to his wife, "if you didn't know that girl had been going through some kind of emotional crisis ever since Miss Flackley's body was found, what would you think of her?"

"I'd think she was having a fight with her boyfriend," she replied at once. "That's been bothering me, too, Peter. One would expect her to act more stoical to show she had nothing to do with Miss Flackley's death, or more agitated because she did. In fact, it would have been quite in line with her recent behavior to stay in her room and sulk. Matilda Gables isn't here. At least I don't see her anywhere."

Matilda's absence didn't necessarily mean anything, of course. Most of the students here were animal husbandry majors. The rest had snatched at an excuse to sleep late after the arduous past two days. Nobody had expected the entire student body to attend; the church wouldn't have held them anyway.

Hjalmar Olafssen was visible, but making no attempt to get near the Svensons. He walked with a group of his buddies, all of them looking down in the mouth. Maybe they were feeling sad about Miss Flackley. Or maybe they were worried about how far the loss of her skill might affect Balaclava's chances at the Competition. She'd shod the whole team last week so the horses would be used to their new footwear when the great day came, but what if one of them cast a shoe at the last minute?

Shandy was shocked to realize the Competition was now but three days away. Normally, Hjalmar and his cohorts would be out training like mad at this very minute. They were all seniors, and this would be their last whack at achieving immortality in the annals of their alma mater. No wonder they were glum.

He could be doing the upperclassmen an injustice. They might well be thinking not of the moment of glory that might be denied them but of Flackley the Farrier in her neat corduroys and bright gardening gloves: brisk, cheerful, competent, a quaint little figure with one gigantic horseshoe in her hand and its mate nailed up on the stall door behind her.

Those horseshoes. Why had they so mysteriously been turned wrong side up immediately before this ghastly thing happened to her? He remembered joking with Helen about them, but he hadn't, down deep, thought it was funny at all. And many a true word was spoken in jest.

What if both the horseshoe switching and the kidnapping of Belinda had in fact been some archcompetitor's fell design to throw Balaclava College into a turmoil and its team off its stride? Was that idea really any crazier than the one he'd had about the Viggies? Was it possibly a good deal saner?

In theory, the Annual Competition was run on pure and lofty amateur principles, with ribbons and trophies the only rewards. In general, that was the case or the college would not have competed. However, betting on the side was not unheard of, and the sums involved might be larger than any but the bettors knew. Shandy had never heard of an attempt to nobble an odds-on favorite, but that wasn't to say it could never happen.

But no competitor, however evil-minded, would kill Flackley the Farrier! Every other team needed her as much as Balaclava's did.

According to the theory he'd been airing to Helen and Iduna at the table last night, Miss Flackley wasn't meant to be killed. If one lot of amateurs could slip up, why couldn't another?

Drat it, he didn't want any more theories. All he wanted was a few plain, simple, irrefutable facts.

They were almost at the cemetery now. He could see the hearse turning in through the rusty iron gates, Frank Flackley in the borrowed college van right behind it. Goulson had wanted Flackley to ride in the funeral parlor's one limousine, but the farrier had opted to drive himself. He'd begged the police to release the family van for the obsequies, offering to return it immediately afterward, but they'd hardheartedly refused.

Or so he'd complained to Iduna when he'd dropped by

earlier to ask if she'd ride in the van with him, on the paltry and improbable excuse that she, being the only other stranger and westerner in town, would be his most appropriate companion. Iduna had quite properly replied that it wouldn't look right, and besides, she wasn't ready yet, so he'd gone alone.

Flackley had tried again outside the church after the service. That had been a serious tactical error. Iduna had been too solicitous for the woe-weighted heart of Professor Stott to do more than shake her head, while Lorene McSpee, who happened to be right behind them, had brushed past with a glad cry of, "Well, if she won't, I will. My feet are killing me. Come on, Professor."

She'd then clambered into the cab, dragging poor old Timothy Ames after her like a rag doll. Shandy felt some satisfaction that the forward Flackley's nostrils were being assailed by the fumes of bleach water, but not much. He didn't like the way this good-looking stranger was hanging around Iduna, trying to snare her away from Tim, who was so desperately in need of rescue from that she-dragon.

Now they were gathering at the Flackley family plot. Now they were taking the coffin from the hearse. Now the pallbearers were carrying it to the freshly dug hole. Now Goulson and his son were heaping the many bouquets and wreaths around. Now the minister was opening his worn-out Bible. Now he was saying the words that had been said over Martha Flackley's father and all the Flackleys before him. Now the Goulsons, father and son, stepped up to deliver their final tribute.

" 'All things bright and beautiful,' " they sang in strong, true harmony, " 'All creatures great and small.' "

"All creatures great and small" could mean to Professor Stott only one great creature and her unborn progeny. The composure he had striven so manfully to maintain now left him. He groped in his overcoat pocket for a clean handkerchief. As he drew it out, a tiny pattering of small, darkish, oval objects fell about his feet. Shandy knew without looking that they were sunflower seeds.

Out of nowhere, Lieutenant Corbin appeared and laid a hand on the department chairman's shoulder.

"Professor Stott," he said quietly, "would you mind just stepping over to the police cruiser for a moment? I'd like a private word with you."

Chapter 16

So deftly was it done that hardly anybody noticed. The service was concluded, the benediction pronounced, the crowd began to disperse. The fact that Stott was already dispersed did not escape Thorkjeld Svenson. Few things ever did. As his wife and Helen stopped to chat, he maneuvered himself to Shandy's side.

"What was that all about?"

Shandy glanced around to make sure nobody was trying to eavesdrop, then he said quietly, "I think Stott's either been or is about to be arrested for murdering Miss Flackley. For God's sake, don't bellow."

"Did he?"

"No."

"Who did?"

"I don't know. I will, soon."

"Make it damn soon," grunted Svenson. "Found out what's wrong with Birgit?"

"Still isn't talking, eh?"

"Not a yip except 'No thank you, I'm not hungry,' and 'Please leave me alone.' I keep telling her she's making a damned fool of herself."

"That ought to soften any daughter's heart," said Shandy. "I have a feeling, however, that she's not. Mind seeing that my wife and her guest get home all right? If you ever succeed in getting a word in edgewise, please explain that I had urgent business elsewhere."

He bummed a ride with somebody or other back to the college, and made a beeline for the girls' dormitories.

Luckily for him, Balaclava clung to the old system of housemothers who kept track of their charges. Within ten minutes, he was face to face with a cowering Matilda Gables.

"I thought you'd be interested to know, Miss Gables," he began without preamble, "that Professor Stott has been arrested for Miss Flackley's murder."

"But—but why?"

"On account of those sunflower seeds you spilled in her van last Friday night while you were sitting there meditating your clever little trick on Birgit Svenson."

"I wasn't meditating anything," cried Matilda. "Not —not then, anyway."

"I see. Only to kiss the air that lately kissèd thee, eh?"

"S-something like that."

"Perhaps we'd better recapitulate. Correct me if I stray from the facts. You attended that dull lecture in the Home Arts Auditorium. You slipped out, probably shortly after Olafsscn and Miss Svenson did. You may or may not have had the intention of spying on them."

"I didn't! Truly I didn't. It was just that the hall was so stuffy and the speaker such a bore, and all the girls around me were holding hands with the boys they were sitting beside, and I—I wasn't sitting beside anybody."

"I see. So you went out, and what to your wondering eyes should appear but the chap you've been worshipping from afar, going at it hot and heavy with the President's daughter in Miss Flackley's van."

Miss Gables nodded miserably.

"Then what did you do?"

"I—I walked off a little way and sat down on a bench. I wasn't spying. I was just—feeling rotten."

"Yes, I daresay you were. Well, you weren't the first and you won't be the last, if that's any consolation, which I don't suppose it is. So then the two lovebirds flew the coop and you went over and sat in the van, right? Making believe."

"Yes, making believe. It sounds so utterly stupid when you say it like that."

"Oh, come now, Miss Gables. There's nothing wrong with imagining things, *per se*. If one didn't preface the reality with the dream, nothing would ever get accomplished. The only complication arises when we—er— dream the impossible dream. You managed somehow to persuade yourself that if Olafssen weren't so totally—er—wrapped up with Birgit Svenson, he might switch his attentions to you. Common sense ought to have told you that no such thing would ever happen."

"But he smiles at me in the library!"

"He smiles at my wife in the library, too. One of Olafssen's charms, which I grant you are many, is his naturally sunny disposition. He smiles at you not because you're Matilda Gables but simply because you're there to be smiled at. In this he differs from Sergeant Lubbock, who smiled at you for—er—definite and specific reasons."

"What reasons?" said Matilda sullenly.

"As the information was imparted in confidence, I do not feel free to repeat it. However, I expect he'd be willing to tell you himself, given the opportunity. Getting back to more immediate subjects, how long did you stay in Miss Flackley's van?"

"Not very long, I shouldn't think. I saw the lights go up in the lecture hall and I knew people would be starting to come out soon, so I split. I—didn't want anybody to see me sitting there by myself. They think I'm whacked out enough already."

"You did have sunflower seeds in your pocket when you got into the van?"

"I suppose so. I generally do. They're rich in natural oils and vitamins and stuff."

"I observed that none of the hulls had been split open, so I gather you weren't munching on them?"

"No, I expect not. Frankly, I don't much care for them. I just keep thinking I ought to."

"That's pretty much how you feel about this college, isn't it?"

Miss Gables sighed. "Since I'm going to be expelled anyway, I might as well say yes."

"Whatever possessed you to come here in the first place?"

"I felt the need to make a contribution to life," she replied primly.

Shandy nodded. "I see. And you thought this was the only kind of contribution that mattered?"

"Well, I knew I'd hate medicine or social work, and how many alternatives are there?"

"How many kinds of work are there?" he snapped back. "What makes you think one job is any more im-

portant than any other? If you're doing something that
makes you miserable, you're apt as not to turn nasty and
try to make somebody else miserable, too. That's what
happened to you Friday night, isn't it? You got to stewing
over why everything went right for Birgit and wrong for
you, and you decided to take Olafssen away from her
to even the score. So then you wrote an anonymous note
and slipped it into her pocket on the way to the assembly
next morning."

The young student looked frightened. "How did you
know?"

"I didn't know, I guessed. Why else would she have
come bouncing down and gone crawling back, and stayed
crying in her room ever since? Get your coat."

Miss Gables turned white as a shirt that had been
washed by Lorene McSpee. "I couldn't."

Shandy considered her. No, he decided, she really
couldn't. The child had been punishing herself as well as
Birgit, and she was on the edge of collapse.

"All right," he said, "I'll do it for you, and I'll try to
keep your name out of it, on one condition."

"What's that?"

"You're to get hold of Sergeant Lubbock and explain
to him how those sunflower seeds got into Miss Flackley's
van. He'll believe you because you left a similar bunch
in his cruiser yesterday afternoon. He probably slept
with them under his pillow last night, if that's any consolation. You don't have to say anything about Olafssen
and Miss Svenson, just that you escaped from a dull lecture and sat in the van because it was handy, that you
had sunflower seeds in your pocket and undoubtedly
spilled some because you always do. You're to say you've
just heard about Professor Stott's being arrested because
he happened to scatter sunflower seeds out of his pocket
today at Miss Flackley's funeral and you're convinced it
was either a coincidence or a deliberate plant. Think you
can manage that much?"

"Oh yes! How can I reach Sergeant Lubbock?"

"Call the state police. Tell them who you are, that
you have evidence that may be important in the Flackley
murder, and that you want Lubbock because you were
with him yesterday and he'll understand what you have
to say better than anyone else. They'll contact him for

you, and you stay glued to the phone until he calls you back. Got that?"

"Yes, Professor Shandy. I'll do it this minute."

"Good. After you've told Lubbock your story, I suggest that you ask if he might spare some time for a discussion of your personal—er—aims and objectives. He had a—er—similar dilemma, he told me, so I think you'll find the conversation—er—productive. Lubbock made Phi Beta Kappa at Dartmouth before attending the police academy, by the way."

"Oh."

There was some color in Miss Gables's cheeks now. "Professor, why are you being so much kinder to me than I deserve?"

"Let's say I want you to have one fond memory of Balaclava. Now get cracking, young woman. You said you wanted to do something useful with your life, and you'll never have a better opportunity."

Matilda took off like a scared pheasant, her hair flying straight out behind her. Shandy checked the housemother's sheet, made sure Matilda had in fact got back to her dormitory shortly after that lecture would have been over, and made his way thence to Valhalla. Again Sieglinde met him at the door.

"Where's Birgit?" he said.

"Back in her room."

"Which way?"

"Come."

She led him up the handsome old staircase, down a long hallway, and knocked at the one bedroom door that was shut.

"Please go away," a muffled voice replied.

"Birgit," said her mother, "Professor Shandy has come to see you. You will not show discourtesy to a guest."

The door stayed shut. Mrs. Svenson knocked more imperiously.

"Birgit!"

Shandy cleared his throat. "Er—Sieglinde, why don't you go along downstairs and let me handle this?"

Being a wise woman, she obeyed. Shandy opened the thinnest blade of his jackknife, did some deft work in the huge iron keyhole, opened the door, and walked in.

"Birgit," he said to the huddle on the bed, "I came to tell you that you've been a dratted fool. I'm ashamed that any student of mine could jump to a false conclusion on the strength of fabricated evidence."

That did it. Birgit shot upright, eyes blazing.

"How dare you talk to me like that in my own bed-room?"

"Where else am I supposed to talk to you if you won't come out?" Shandy asked reasonably. "Where's that note?"

"What note?"

"Dissimulation is not your strong suit, young woman. Hand it over."

"I burned it," she muttered.

"Then you did another stupid thing, and you ought to be even more ashamed of yourself. Never mind. I can approximate what it said. Something to the effect that while you knew what Olafssen was doing with you in Flackley the Farrier's van during the lecture, you'd never guess what he was doing with whom later on, and there was no sense in asking him because he wouldn't tell you. Right?"

Birgit did not reply.

"Answer me," he barked.

She nodded as though her head were being shoved from behind by a stronger hand.

"More or less."

"And because the note turned up in your pocket at the assembly, you assumed it referred to your young man's being instrumental in stealing the van, kidnapping Belinda, and murdering Miss Flackley. Right?"

"I—I couldn't believe—"

"Then why didn't you say so instead of throwing a fit of the megrims and worrying your parents half to death?"

"But we—we were in the van."

"I know you were. Doing what came naturally. Nothing criminal about that, is there?"

"Mother might not agree with you."

"Don't underestimate your mother, young woman. How do you think she managed to have seven kids of her own?"

Birgit emitted a feeble giggle. The tide of battle was turning.

"If you'd used your head," Shandy went on, "it might have occurred to you that you were observed in your—er—occupation by a fellow student who, like a good

many others around here, happens to suffer an unre-
quited passion for Hjalmar Olafssen. This young person
got into the van after you left it, and sat brooding on the
injustice of a fate that threw Olafssen into your arms instead of hers. She continued to brood, probably through
a more or less sleepless night, and arose in the small hours
with a plan straight out of *Othello*.

"She penned that clever epistle, worded so as to plant
the seed of doubt, with the intention of slipping it to you
whenever she got a chance. Unfortunately, opportunity
presented itself before she'd had a chance to regret her
crackbrained impulse. Your father called a general assembly. Did you know what it was about?"

"Yes, I did."

Birgit was talking without reluctance now. "As you
perhaps know, Professor Stott came banging on the door
at some ungodly hour and woke us all up with the news
that Belinda was missing. After that we didn't sleep
much. My kid sisters got to acting silly, so Mama decided
we might as well go downstairs and have breakfast. Then
Papa decided he'd better stroll over to the pigpens and
see what was happening. A while later he phoned to say
they'd found Miss Flackley dead, that he was calling a
general assembly, and that I'd better show up since I'm
a student. I got dressed and ran to the athletic field. Naturally, my nose started running as soon as I sat down
—you know how it does when you've been rushing
around in the cold—so I reached in my pocket hoping
I'd brought a tissue, and found that note. Then I— Well,
under the circumstances, what would anybody have
thought?"

"I'll grant you the timing was damnably unfortunate.
The poor little jughead meant only to suggest that your
boyfriend was seeing another girl. Knowing your—er—
impetuous temperament, she entertained the fantasy that
you'd hand him the mitten forthwith and he'd go dashing
to her for solace because he'd smiled at her in the library
once or twice. She stuck the note in your pocket as you
were climbing into the bleachers. By the time she learned
what the meeting was about and realized you might make
the wrong interpretation, it was too late to take her little
bombshell back. She's horrified by what she's done, of
course."

"She darn well ought to be," said Birgit. "You see,

Professor, the awful part of it was that Hjalmar and I had actually been joking out there in the van about stealing Belinda's piglets and hiding them somewhere till we could train them to become useful citizens. You remember that paper he wrote?"

"I do. So when the pig disappeared, you thought he'd gone ahead and done it, eh?"

"Wouldn't you? Hjalmar does get these sudden impulses at times. Then when I found the note and heard about Miss Flackley—well, you know what a klutz he is. I couldn't really picture Hjalmar stuffing her body into the mash feeder and going off in the van with Belinda, but—" She flung wide her hands.

"So you thought you could solve the problem by throwing a tantrum."

"I didn't think at all! Not at first, anyway. I just went into shock. Then I thought I'd better stay that way. If I simply refused to say anything to anybody, I couldn't get him into trouble."

"Shut your mouth and pray for a miracle, eh?"

"Yes, and it worked! You're it! Oh, Professor Shandy, how can I ever thank you?"

She hurtled from the bed, flung her arms around his neck, and gave him a tremendous smack on the cheek.

"M' well, that ought to do for a start," he replied. "Now I suggest you go downstairs and explain to your mother. Then you'd better patch things up with Hjalmar and go help hunt for Belinda. You—er—don't harbor any latent destructive tendencies toward her, I trust?"

"Of course not! I'm against pork breeding on principle, but I wouldn't harm darling Belinda for a billion dollars. Professor Stott adores her. My gosh, practically the first thing I can remember is sitting on his lap while he played 'This little piggie goes to market' with my toes. He's marvelous with children, you know. My oldest sister, Karin, was a great friend of his daughters. Mary Beth, Julie Beth, Clara Beth, and Lily Beth were over here all the time, or else we were over at their house bumming cookies off Mrs. Stott. She was the most fabulous cook! I cried buckets at her funeral. I've never cried so much since, until now. And to think it was on account of some goggle-eyed little— Oh, oh! I'll bet I can guess who she is."

"I'll bet you're going to have sense enough to keep your guesses to yourself," said Shandy. "In any event, the

—er—person in question will not be among us much longer. She never belonged here in the first place."

"Does Papa know?"

"He soon will. Now go and apologize to your parents for being such a—er—klutz. If any of your classmates should ask embarrassing questions, I'd—invent a slight case of wheat germ poisoning or something of the sort to account for your recent inactivity. You are now fully recovered and ready to do your share. There's plenty to do. You may not be aware that Professor Stott has been detained for questioning in the death of Miss Flackley."

"Professor Stott? But that's crazy! We'll picket the jail till they let him out."

"Atta girl," said Shandy. "Well, then, I'll—er—leave you to it."

Chapter 17

Sieglindo was standing at the foot of the stairs, her face strained.

"Well, Peter?"

"Birgit will be down in a minute. She's just going to dab a little cold water on her eyes, then organize a posse to march on the county hoosegow and liberate Stott."

"Ah, then she is back to normal and will no doubt be in jail herself by nightfall. Thank you, Peter."

"My pleasure. If you need bail money, let me know."

"Will you not stay for coffee?"

"Thanks, but I'd better organize a march on my wife and explain why I left her waiting at the church."

Shandy left Valhalla and took the long path that led down through the campus to the Crescent. There was hardly anybody around. The students, once Professor Stott's calamity had become public knowledge, had surged forth with renewed fervor to find his pig for him. One belated searcher, struggling into his mackinaw even as he spoke, explained prevailing student opinion to Shandy in a few trenchant words:

"I mean, jeez, we've got oddballs around here I wouldn't let within ten feet of me with a salad fork, but Old Lardface—I mean Professor Stott—I mean, jeez!"

"Those sentiments do you credit, young man," Shandy had replied. "Carry on with all zeal, and may your efforts be rewarded."

His next encounter was less welcome. Mirelle Feldster, tippytoeing up the path in high-heeled boots that must

151

have put a severe strain on her pudgy ankles, managed
to spread herself so he couldn't possibly get by without
knocking her down.

"Oh, Peter," she cried, "isn't this too dreadful for
words! Do you think they'll have restored the death pen-
alty before he comes to trial, or will he get away with
life imprisonment?"

"If you're talking about the person who planted that
false evidence on Stott this morning," he replied levelly,
"I daresay the sentence will be somewhat less drastic. I
shouldn't be too worried if I were you, Mirelle."

He left her, for once, speechless and went on his way.
As he walked, he began to wonder. He'd meant only to
wipe that smirk off her silly face and shut her up. In
that effort, he'd miraculously succeeded, but perhaps he'd
done something more.

Jim Feldster had been connected with Balaclava for
a great many years, much longer than Peter Shandy.
He'd come there as a teaching fellow in Fundamentals
of Dairy Management. He was now a full professor, still
teaching Fundamentals of Dairy Management. He taught
the subject ably, conscientiously, and, as far as anybody
knew, contentedly.

Feldster was no nonentity in his profession. He had
published a meticulously researched monograph on The
History of Cream Separation. He had delivered a paper
to the National Dairymen's Association, excerpts from
which were printed in the *Balaclava County Weekly
Fane and Pennon,* along with a picture of Professor
Feldster being congratulated by several dairy dignitaries
for his significant contribution to the subject of Butterfat
Content.

In his younger days, Jim had won firsts in several important milking contests. Now it was his pleasure to
stand nearby beaming with quiet pride as his students in
turn basked in their moment of teat-stripping glory. He
was withal as good a teacher of Fundamentals of Dairy
Management as any institution of higher learning could
want. On the few occasions when he'd been asked to do
anything else, he'd been an utter washout.

Notwithstanding his years of seniority and his respected position in the college community, Jim Feldster
had about as much chance of taking over Stott's job as
Shandy had of being elected Pope. Why should Jim have

wanted it? He had his cows and his clubs. He knew more passwords, rituals, and secret handshakes than anybody else in Balaclava County, with the possible exception of Harry Goulson. He'd carved out his niche, and Shandy would have sworn he was content to stay in it.

Not so his wife. If Jim had reached the pinnacle of his ambition, Mirelle assuredly had not. She craved more than a polite greeting at a faculty banquet. She wanted to be up there in the receiving line, right next to Sieglinde Svenson.

Mirelle had been standing close to Stott during the final rites at the grave. She must know about the sunflower seeds that had been found in Miss Flackley's abandoned van. Stott himself might have mentioned the curious little circumstance to his colleague, and Jim had passed it on to Mirelle simply because it seemed so unimportant. Shandy knew that Jim often did ramble on to his wife about trivia so that she wouldn't be continually accusing him of never letting her in on the latest faculty gossip.

Mirelle probably had sunflower seeds in the house. Everybody around the Crescent fed birds. She'd be asinine enough to think she'd be furthering Jim's career by cramming a handful into Stott's pocket, and she was nosy enough to have noticed that Stott did keep a clean handkerchief there. If he hadn't produced the linen at the right moment, she could always have pretended she'd forgotten her own and asked to borrow his.

Remembering the way she'd come spouting venom all over his own living room night before last, Shandy thought it not at all impossible that Mirelle would progress from malicious gossip to malicious action if the effort were not too great and she thought she could get away with it. He wondered if it was possible to fingerprint sunflower seeds. Most likely she'd been wearing gloves. Helen or Iduna might know.

He quickened his pace toward home, but snarled as he came in sight of the Crescent and spied the borrowed college van all but blocking the narrow roadway in front of the brick house. Frank Flackley was there again, looking for sympathy and various other things, no doubt. Why wasn't he out shoeing a horse? Why wasn't he back at Forgery Point, brooding over the family album? Why wasn't he anywhere but here?

If Flackley sensed that he was unwelcome, he certainly didn't show it. Clutching a half-empty glass of beer, he made a token gesture at rising from Shandy's favorite chair.

"Howdy, Professor."

"Er—howdy," Shandy replied. "Sorry to be so late, Helen. I was—er—detained. I gather you're taking the day off, Flackley?"

"Nope, just hiding out," the farrier replied affably. "I dunno's you noticed, Professor, but I met me a hungry woman back there at the funeral. I don't mind bein' friendly, but there's limits to what a man's nose can stand. Bein' around a rodeo ain't no bunch of violets, but you don't generally have to put up with sittin' next to somebody that smells like a pay toilet in a bus station, if the ladies'll excuse my language. I give her and the old geezer a ride home because he looked like he needed one, but when she says to me, 'Come in for coffee,' I says, 'Sorry, I got urgent business elsewhere.' "

He took a rather self-satisfied pull at his drink. "So then I seen Miz Shandy and Miss Iduna here comin' up the walk and I figured they wouldn't be hardhearted enough to turn away a poor orphan boy. Goulson sure gave Aunt Martha a royal send-off, didn't he? I told him I'd do a little tinkerin' on that old hearse of his to make up. Don't know as you noticed, but she's gettin' kind of weak in the joints."

"No, I didn't notice," said Shandy. "I'd have said the hearse was in excellent condition."

"Yeah, but you ain't been around wagons like I have," Flackley replied. "That was part of my job when I worked for Rudy. Of course we didn't travel by wagon, but we had a couple we used in the show. You know, the Old-Timer rattlin' along in the chuck wagon with pots and pans whangin' and bangin', stuff like that. Them wagons took an awful beatin'. Many's the night I've worked straight through, forgin' new parts and I don't know what all, so's we'd be ready to roll for the next day's show. Then like as not I'd have to daub flour on my hair and beard an' play the Old-Timer because the guy that was s'posed to drive the wagon was off on a toot. That's how come I grew this bush. Never knew when Rudy was goin' to need some hairy-faced ol' desert rat in a hurry, an' it was easier than havin' to glue one on."

"You're a man of many parts, Flackley," said his host somewhat dryly.

"Yeah, well, that's show biz, like they say. Now that I'm settlin' down an' turnin' respectable, I been kind o' wonderin' whether I ought to get me a shave. What do you think, Miss Iduna?"

The comely blonde looked at Flackley, to Shandy's secret joy, as if she couldn't remember who he was.

"I'm sorry, I just can't think of anything but poor Professor Stott. You don't suppose that policeman would be foolish enough to arrest him, do you?"

"I thought they already had," said the farrier petulantly. "Took him away in the cruiser, didn't they?"

"That was just for questioning," Shandy insisted. "Routine procedure."

"Darn funny they'd pull their routine in the middle of Aunt Martha's funeral."

Flackley set down his empty glass and rose. "Well, folks, it's sure been nice talkin' to you. Thanks for the beer. Don't s'pose you got a wagon that needs fixin', but if there's any odd jobs you'd like done around the house, just let me know. I'd like to do somethin' to pay you back after all you done for me."

"Er—thank you," said Shandy. "We'll—er—bear your offer in mind. I expect you'll be extremely busy for a while, however, catching up on back work, and so on."

"Don't look that way. Aunt Martha seems to have got pretty well caught up before she was killed. I guess on account of this here little show you folks are havin' everybody wanted their horses shod in advance. I got nothin' scheduled for the next few days except a few odds an' ends. That's why I thought I'd work on Mr. Goulson's hearse tomorrow, to keep myself busy an' get the feel of the old forge. You folks take a run out. I'll buy the beer."

"Thanks, we may do that."

Shandy got the unwanted guest outside and refrained by a valiant effort of will from slamming the door behind him. Then he returned to the women.

"Has there been any word about Stott?"

"Not yet," Helen told him. "Peter, we're worried sick."

"We've been wondering," Iduna ventured with unaccustomed diffidence, "if they'd let us go and see him. Maybe take him a few doughnuts or something to hearten him up."

"Oh, I doubt if they'll detain him long," said Shandy. "Those sunflower seeds in his pocket were an obvious plant, and I have a sneaky hunch who planted them, and why. Furthermore, they were a waste of time, because that lot found in the van had nothing to do with the murder. Lieutenant Corbin probably has the whole story by now, but I think I'll see if I can get hold of him and make sure. By the way, you may be interested to know that our band of Vigilant Vegetarians will soon be reduced by one member, and that Birgit Svenson is out storming the barricades again."

"Well, well," said Helen. "So that's the way the tofu crumbles? Do hurry and telephone Lieutenant Corbin, Peter. I simply can't bear to think of Professor Stott's being subjected to such a ridiculous humiliation."

"Me, neither," Iduna added with such feeling that Shandy looked at her in wonderment before he went to make the call.

The telephone was in his minuscule office. From force of habit, he sat down at his desk to use the instrument, noting with a surprising lack of interest that he'd forgotten to water a flat of seedlings he'd started under the Gro-lite in there, and that they were looking rather sick. He came out of the office looking far sicker than his seedlings.

"They know about the sunflower seeds, and they're discounting them as evidence," he told the women. "Unfortunately, while they were examining his overcoat, they found a few small bloodstains around the pocket."

"Oh, my stars!" cried Iduna. "But couldn't they be— mightn't he have cut his finger, or—"

Shandy shook his head. "Stott's blood type is AB. The stains are type O."

"But O is the commonest type there is," Helen sputtered. "Half the people in the world are type O."

"True, and Miss Flackley happened to be among the majority."

"But—but wasn't he wearing a different coat that night?"

"Helen, how many good dark overcoats do I possess?"

"One," she mumbled.

"And how many would you assume any man on this faculty owns? Stott's no fashion plate, any more than the rest of us. Besides, he's already admitted it's the same coat, though he is totally at a loss as to how the blood-stains got on it. End of quote."

"Well, I'd explain it fast enough if I were that cop," Iduna blazed. "I'd hunt up every last person who was at that funeral and see which of them is wearing a Band-Aid on his hand. Stands to reason the person who bled on his coat's the same one who crammed those sunflower seeds into his pocket, doesn't it? Where's that Lieutenant Corbin's phone number, Peter? I'll soon give him a piece of my mind. A fine, upstanding man like Professor Stott!"

The Shandys regarded each other thoughtfully. At last Peter shook his head.

"Frankly, Iduna, I don't think that's a terribly good idea. I don't mean about the Band-Aid. I think you have an excellent point there, and I'll be happy to pass your suggestion along to the state police myself. The problem is, there's already been—er—talk about Stott and Miss Flackley, and while we know it's totally unfounded, there might be—er—conjectures if you were to enter the lists as his champion. Especially if you went over there lugging him doughnuts. Right now, you can best help Stott by lying low and keeping dark."

Miss Bjorklund tossed her curls angrily. "Fine doings, I must say, when a person can't—can't even—" Her face crumpled, and she began to cry.

Helen stood on tiptoe to put her arms around as much of her friend as she could encompass. "Iduna, please don't take it so hard. Peter will get him out. Everything will be all right. You'll see."

Shandy cleared his throat, wishing he could produce words that would stem that Niagara of tears. All he could think of was, "Now, now. I know it's tough on you," though why it should be tougher on her than on the rest of them was more than he could comprehend.

"I'm sorry if I was tactless, but, Iduna, you must realize that you're a fine figure of a woman and Stott hasn't been exactly blind to that fact. The police must have seen you two together at the funeral." How could they have missed?

"He—he said I was the star that illumined his dark night of tribulation," she sniffled. "How the heck am I supposed to illumine if I can't so much as slap him together a couple of sandwiches?"

"Can't you—er—shine from afar? It won't be for long, Iduna, I promise you."

"How Shandy intended to keep that promise, he hadn't the remotest idea. He hoped Iduna wouldn't press him for details. As it happened, she didn't get a chance. At that moment, Thorkjeld Svenson entered, not bothering to knock but merely wresting the massive solid oak door loose from its hinges and tossing it into the shrubbery.

"For Yesus' sake, come quick, Shandy," he bellowed. "They've vandalized the wagon!"

Chapter 18

"Great balls of fire!"

Professor Shandy stared at his President in horror and dismay. Although the college possessed a number of horse-drawn conveyances, including the venerated one-horse chaise in which Balaclava Buggins himself had driven around the country lanes trying to scout up students for his about-to-be-founded Agricultural College, he knew at once which wagon Svenson meant.

It was the huge dray which from the beginning of history—Competition history, at any rate—had transported the mighty men and sometimes mightier women of Balaclava to the county fairgrounds and back. It was the wagon that, with eight gargantuan Balaclava Blacks hitched four abreast, had led each opening-day procession around the exhibition ring, with the Balaclava Boosters' Drum and Bugle Band whanging and blatting and making a glorious racket that sent the audience into cheering frenzy. It was the wagon that every man, woman, and child in Balaclava County, not excepting the haughty Hoddersvillites and those stuck-up snobs from Lumpkin Corners, waited all year long to see.

Cripes, thought Shandy, no wonder the President had ripped off that front door with his bare hands. Under these circumstances, it was the natural and reasonable thing to do. Pausing only to grab his mackinaw and suggest that Helen get hold of a carpenter from Buildings and Grounds before she and Iduna froze to death, he set off for the wagon barns at a speed he hadn't shown since the summer of 1961, when an Aberdeen Angus bull had taken umbrage at his entering the pasture in a plaid flannel shirt of the wrong clan tartan.

The wagon was an appalling sight. One wheel was off. The poles were on the floor, their couplings smashed to bits. Around them lay several of the beer kegs that served for band seats, their staves kicked in and their iron hoops bent as by blows from a sledgehammer.

Shandy, who knew a great deal more about wagons than Flackley had given him credit for, took careful inventory. The damage was somewhat less catastrophic than it had looked at first glance, but cunningly contrived to be the sort that no college maintenance man could hope to put right.

Svenson picked up one of the damaged oaken kegs, cradling it to his mammoth bosom as a mother would her baby. "Yiminy, Shandy, what are we going to do?"

"I suppose we ought to call the police," said the professor not very enthusiastically.

"Yah, and they take away the pieces for evidence and we get'em back maybe six years from now. Shandy, you yackass, we show up at the Competition without our wagon, everybody says the college is falling apart. We start losing students. Instead of good farmers, America gets lousy computer programmers. The fate of the nation is at stake and you say call the cops!"

"President, shut up," Shandy replied wearily. "I didn't say do it, I only said we ought to, which you know as well as I. As to the insanity of such a course, I couldn't agree with you more. What we need is—by jingo, Flackley! He was up at the house not half an hour ago, spouting off about how he used to have to make emergency repairs on the rodeo wagons."

"Yah, but was he telling the truth?"

"How the flaming perdition do I know? Either we let him try or we get hold of a medium and resurrect old Matt Flackley. He was the last one to work on it, wasn't he?"

"Yesus, yes! Maybe they still have some spare parts up at the forge. At least Flackley should have the right tools. Find him!"

"I'll do my best. He may be over at Harry Goulson's. He said he'd promised to do some work on—"

"Arrgh!" said Svenson.

Shandy realized this was no time for conversation. Still traveling at a lively clip, he headed for Main Street.

Flackley was there. Shandy could see the van parked not at Goulson's but in front of the Ruptured Duck, Balaclava Junction's one feeble excuse for a restaurant. He went in and found the farrier perched on a stool at the counter, shoveling in an appalling mess of deep-fried objects that had perhaps started out as edible foodstuffs. Flackley waved his fork with easy friendliness.

"Hi, Professor, haul up a stool an' set. Buy you a cup o' coffee?"

"Er—no, thank you."

Shandy lowered his voice. "The fact is, we've run into a—er—little problem up at the barns, and we need you right away."

"Sure thing. Got time to finish my grub here? I never et no breakfast, an' my guts was startin' to growl."

"You should have said so when you were at the house. My wife would have given you something other than beer and cheese."

"You folks done enough for me already."

Flackley bolted the rest of the loathesome agglomeration on his plate with frightening rapidity, tossed a bill on the counter, said, "Thanks, Mabel, see you later," to the waitress, and followed Shandy outdoors.

"Now, Professor," he said as they climbed into the van, "what's this little problem of yours?"

"Actually, it's a big problem," Shandy confessed, "and I'm hoping to God you can help us out. You see, the college owns a very large old wagon that we take to the Competition every year."

"Oh yeah, Aunt Martha mentioned that. Didn't my great-grandfather forge the hardware, or something?"

"Various Flackleys have worked on the wagon over the years. Anyway, President Svenson just went to check it over, and found that it's been vandalized."

"Jeez, that's terrible! You folks sure have been havin' a run of hard luck around here. When did it happen?"

"Sometime during the night, I expect. Actually, we're not sure. With so many of us out hunting for the pig and the rest trying to fill in for them here, there, and everywhere, I doubt if anybody's been into the wagon barns for the past couple of days. In any event, the Competition starts day after tomorrow, and we absolutely must have the big dray in shape to roll by then."

"Sounds like the old days with Rudy," Flackley grunted. "Don't sweat it, Professor."

He gunned the college van and got them to the barns in no time flat. President Svenson was still there, standing among the ruins like Samson at Gaza. Flackley hopped out and started poking about while they waited with bated breath for his diagnosis.

At last the farrier, straightened up, wiped his hands on the seat of his pants, and pronounced his verdict.

"Well, I seen worse."

"Never mind you seen," said Svenson. "'How about you fixed?"

"Lemme think a minute. You need the wagon first thing in the morning, day after tomorrow. Right?"

"Wrong. We need it tomorrow six P.M. We drive to the fairgrounds, six hours, rest the horses midnight to seven, feed and water, harness up, and we're heading the parade at nine o'clock on the button."

"That makes it tight. But don't sweat it, Mr. President. I don't get no sleep between now and then, that's all. See, I was out checkin' around the old smithy. There's plenty to work with up there, even extry hoops for these here barrels. They part of the rig?"

"They're what the band sits on," Shandy explained. "You see, they screw into these iron flanges so they won't tip and send the buglers tail over crupper into the drums, giving rise to general discord and bucolic ribaldry."

"Yeah, well, they're no great problem. Look, if you can find a towrope and a crew to raise the wagon so's I can get this wheel back on, I'll hitch'er to the van and get'er back to the forge. Once I'm there, I think I can promise to have the wagon ready for the show. I won't say it'll be a real classy job, but she'll hold together. That's what counts, ain't it? I expect you got some bunting or somethin' you can drape around to hide the gouges. That's what Rudy always done."

"Oh yes," Shandy assured him. "We've got a whole committee appointed to gussy the thing up. Now, let's start on this wheel."

"You mean you an' him?"

"We've done messier jobs than this. Right, President?"

"Right."

Thorkjeld bent double and hoisted the sagging corner of the enormous dray on his own back. "Make it snappy, Flackley. I'm not as young as I used to be."

"Jeez," said the farrier reverently. Then he got to work.

As he'd said himself, Flackley wasn't fancy but he was certainly fast. Though he appeared somewhat shaken at having to use a college president for a jack, he got the wheel back on the axle and within half an hour pronounced the wagon safe to travel.

Soon a little procession was winding its way toward Forgery Point: Flackley driving the college van, Svenson riding in the drag to keep an eye on the towropes or go down with his ship as the case might be, and Shandy following in his own car to guard the rear and pick up any pieces that fell off en route. The trip was maddeningly slow since they didn't dare joggle the disabled wagon any more than was absolutely necessary, but they got there. Flackley jumped from the van and started to loosen the hitches.

"Okay, gents, if you'll help me shove 'er around to the smithy, I'll take 'er from here."

"We'll be glad to stay and pump the bellows, or whatever," Shandy offered, but Flackley shook his head.

"Thanks, but to tell the truth, you'd only be in my way. Tell you what would be a big help, though. Could you bring the horses out here tomorrow night instead of me having to tow the wagon back? The Seven Forks is more or less on the way to the fairgrounds anyway, ain't it? That'd shorten your trip some an' give me a couple of extry hours if I need 'em."

"President, I think Flackley has an excellent point there," said Shandy. "We can bring the band this far by bus easily enough."

"Yeah, sure," said Flackley, "long as it ain't too big a bus. That sure is an awful stretch of road between here an' the Seven Forks. I was kind o' worried about that ol' wagon pitchin' over them potholes, I don't mind tellin' you, even with no load aboard."

"Right," said Svenson. "Bounced like hell. Disgrace to the township. We'll send 'em the whole way by bus."

"That'd be a big load off my mind," said Flackley. "So there'll just be the handlers, eh? How many?"

"Damned if I know. Depends on who's alive and out of jail. Two, three, maybe."

"Great! Then I'll be expectin' you with the horses sometime around eight o'clock tomorrow night. If you want to come out anytime tomorrow to make sure we're gettin' along okay, I'll be glad to have you. Right now I guess I better start firin' up that old forge."

Since Flackley was so obviously anxious to get rid of them, they went. As they got into Shandy's car and started back, Svenson grunted.

"One off the list, anyway."

"Two," said Shandy. "Birgit's talking again."

He explained. Svenson heaved a sigh of relief that almost blew the windshield out.

"Yeepers creepers! And some yackasses go around wishing they could be young again. I knew that Gables kid would cause trouble sooner or later. Didn't want to come here. Acted on principle. Bad business. Turns'em ugly. Next thing you know, they're putting bombs in baby carriages."

"Oh, I doubt if Miss Gables would ever go that far," said Shandy. "Anyway, if that agreeable young chap Lubbock has his way, I expect she'll be—er—putting something else into a baby carriage one of these days."

"Hope so. Usually it's the brainy ones who don't and the brainless who do. If Stott ran his piggery the way we humans run our race, I'd have given him the boot twenty years ago. Where the hell is that animal, Shandy?"

"President, when I find out you'll be the first to know. I can tell you a few thousand places she's not, if that's any help."

"No."

They fell silent. Neither had eaten any lunch, and the afternoon was now far spent. Both were yearning to go home, have a drink and a snack, and take a snooze before dinner.

But Stott's name, now that it had been uttered, lay in the air like a bomb in a baby carriage. When they got out to the Seven Forks, Shandy stopped at the unsavory general store and used the pay phone. Then he swung the car toward the main highway that led to the county lockup.

When they got there, they were refused permission to see the prisoner. With some difficulty, Shandy managed to persuade Svenson not to wrench off the steel bars that prevented their gaining access to their colleague, and asked if Stott had been allowed to contact a lawyer. He was told Professor Stott did not want a lawyer. He could well believe it. Stott would think an honest man did not need a lawyer. The police would think Stott was a nut.

"Then just tell him Shandy and Svenson stopped in to say hello," he told the man at the desk sadly, and they went away.

Chapter 19

By the time Shandy got home, he was feeling lower than a snake's garters. The sight of Iduna's face didn't cheer him any. She must, he thought, be coming down with something. Maybe he was, too. He took the drink Helen handed him and crouched close to the fireplace. The chill seemed to have got into his bones, even though some people had been making asinine remarks about spring in the air. How could they have spring, till Stott was sprung?

Although dinner was no doubt up to standard, Shandy didn't enjoy it much. Timothy Ames dropped over for another round of cribbage afterward, and he didn't particularly enjoy that, either. He felt as though they were all inept actors in a bad play, going through the motions without being able to put any zip into the performance.

As soon as Professor Ames was out the door, Iduna said dully, "If you folks don't mind, I think I'll go to bed."

She looked as if she might be planning to cry herself to sleep, and Shandy was about ready to do the same. Before long, he and Helen followed her upstairs.

Sleep, however, eluded them both. They lay together, not in the mood for what they would normally have been in the mood for, hashing things over. Shandy had told her and Iduna all about the vandalized wagon at the dinner table, but he hadn't dared mention the visit to the lockup for fear of opening the floodgates again. He told Helen now.

"And he won't have a lawyer?" she yawned. "That's understandable. His strength is as the strength of ten because his heart is pure."

166

"Yes, but is purity going to bail him out?" said Shandy.

"Of course. Virtue always triumphs sooner or later. Look at Jane Eyre."

"Why should I? What brought her into the conversation, anyway?"

"I was reading that biography of Charlotte Brontë this afternoon. Oh, by the way, I was wrong about the Bells."

"What bells?"

"Currer, Ellis, and Acton, of course. Remember when we were having that shemozzle about the Buggins Collection and I said I thought six copies of their poems were sold? Actually, there were only two."

"Gad, woman, you do think of the oddest things at the oddest times. How could there have been only two if a copy turned up at Balaclava a hundred and thirty years later?"

"Peter dearest, two copies sold doesn't mean two books in circulation. Charlotte sent copies around to everybody she'd ever heard of, more or less, and they must have kept a few kicking around the house even after they'd sold the rest to that trunkmaker. Authors always do."

"So?"

"So the most logical explanation is that Branwell lugged an armload down to the local pub one night when he was on the sauce and handed them out to the boys in the back room. Mr. Buggins happened to be passing through Haworth at the time—"

"Mr. Buggins of Balaclava County? Come on!"

"He was doing the Grand Tour. They did in those days. Spent a year abroad exploring the picturesque nooks and crannies of the old world and the rest of their lives boring people to death with their souvenirs."

"Haworth wasn't a picturesque nook or cranny."

"Mr. Buggins wouldn't know that, would he? He'd never been there before. Anyway, as I was trying to say, he was in the pub that night and Branwell gave him a book, which he added to his trunkful of mementos."

"Um. What's the second most logical explanation?"

"The trunkmaker, I should think. How do we know he used all the books lining trunks? Maybe his wife thought a few tastefully displayed volumes would add a touch of class to the front parlor. Maybe his—Aha, I have it! He had an apprentice, who was made to sleep on a straw pallet in the workroom, as apprentices invariably were. This apprentice swiped a sufficient number of books to put under his pallet and keep out the drafts from the floor. Paper is an excellent insulator, you know. Then a year or so later when *Jane Eyre* was published and became an overnight success, still under the name of Currer Bell, you must remember, and Ellis and Acton also got their novels printed, the apprentice realized he might be sleeping on something of value. So he fished the books out from under the pallet and peddled them to a second-hand bookseller."

"To buy a noggin of rum," said Shandy idly. Then suddenly he bounded out of bed and reached for his trousers.

"By George, Helen, you've hit it on the noggin!"

Before his wife could say, "Where are you going?" he was gone.

If Helen Shandy had not been so tired herself, she might have got up and followed. Instead, she fell asleep. She did not know that she spent the entire night alone. She did not know why her husband, looking exhausted but jubilant, made his way to Valhalla in the gray light of dawn to find Thorkjeld Svenson, wrapped in a bathrobe, scowling into a coffee mug the size of a washbasin. Nor did she know that when Peter left the mansion on the hill, Thorkjeld Svenson was already upstairs girding his loins for battle and bellowing an ancient Viking war chant.

" 'Down in a meady in a itty bitty pool fam fee itty fitties anna mama fitty too.' Birgit, up! General assembly seven o'clock, all hands on deck; this means you. Sieglinde, breakfast! Much breakfast! This is a day that will live in infamy."

"So why celebrate?" said his wife, going down in her sky-blue robe to do the bidding of her lord, although she knew perfectly well who was master and so did he. "Of infamy we have already enough."

"True, my wife. Oh, 'boomp! Boomp! Diddum, daddum, waddum choo!' "

"Children, I hope you feel due gratitude to your father for rearing you in an atmosphere of culture and refinement. No, Thorkjeld, ham and sausage together you may not have. And less sugar on the porridge. I presume you will in due course inform us as to what this brouhaha is all about."

"Urgh!" said Svenson as he bent with a will to the fueling of the inner man. "Birgit, call the dorms. Get'em up. Athletic field bleachers seven o'clock; no excuses for absence."

"Papa, are you going to announce that we've got Belinda back?"

"No."

"Are you going to tell us Professor Stott is out of jail?"

"No."

"Are you—"

"Go!"

Birgit went.

By the time she got back to the table, her father had already finished breakfast and was losing an argument with his wife about wearing his knitted ski cap.

"Thirty percent of the body heat is lost through the top of the head," Sieglinde insisted. "You will keep your cap on. If not, you will catch the sniffles and set a bad example for the student body."

"Then I'll wear the red one Birgit gave me with the big white doodad on top," said the President sulkily.

"You will not address the college with a doodad on top. You will wear the gray one that matches your sweater and you will behave as a man of dignity. What time will you be home?"

"Who knows?"

Svenson jammed the cap down over his ears and marched for the door. " 'Hi ho, hi ho, it's off to war we go!' "

"Mama, how do you stand him?" demanded Frideswiede, youngest of the seven sisters.

Her father counterwheeled, snatched his wife in a Rudolph Valentino embrace, and bussed her mightily. " 'Farewell, my own. I return with my shield,' or— What the hell's the rest of it?"

"For you there is no rest of it," said his helpmeet, tucking back a strand of flaxen hair and casting a somewhat complacent glance at Frideswiede. "Go, then, I will keep a herring in the window for you."

"Mama," said Gudrun, the second youngest, "it's a candle you're supposed to keep in the window."

"Nonsense, my child. A candle would smoke up the glass and drip on the sill. A herring lies looking mournful and bereft. The symbolism is much more meaningful.

Also it comes in handy for smorgasbord later. Get ready now at once or you will miss the school bus."

At seven o'clock, every student was again in the bleachers. Having been given a little advance warning this time, most of them had managed to get their clothes on. All, needless to say, were agog. Whispers of, "What's he going to say?" circulated madly through the stands. The consensus was that either Belinda or another body had been found, but their President surprised them, as was his wont.

"Tomorrow," he thundered, "we enter the Competition. You know that. You've trained for it. Now you're going to win it!"

Roars of, "You said it, Pres!", "Right on!", and "Let's hear it for King Kong!" filled the air. He held up a hand for silence.

"Later we cheer. Today we work."

"But what about Belinda?" somebody yelled.

"You have heard rumors," Svenson yelled back, "that our sow was pignapped by subversive elements trying to sabotage our chances at the Competition. Now I must tell you that our wagon has been vandalized!"

Howls of outrage rent the air. Again Svenson quelled the tumult.

"Shut up and listen! The wagon is being repaired. It will be ready to roll tonight. It damn well better be," he added in an aside to Shandy, "or I'll nail Flackley's hide to the chapel door." The President was a keen scholar of ancient Viking customs.

"The wagon is at Flackley's smithy, up at Forgery Point," he went on. "There will be no time to bring it back here for the customary Grand Send-off. Also, to prevent undue strain, only the handlers will ride in it to the fairgrounds. The band will travel by bus early tomorrow morning. Today the band will practice, shine the tuba, get ready. Get readier than you've ever been before. You're going to make your entrance on schedule tomorrow morning, and you're going to make it good!"

He glared around. "Wagon trimmers, there will be no chance for you to spend all day arguing over how to drape the bunting as usual. You'll have one hour tomorrow morning at the fairgrounds. Today you organize like Jacques Cousteau going out to photograph a Loch Ness monster. Whatever you need, you get together. There will be no run back to the dorm, Genevieve, and get me a pair of scissors I can cut with. Think! Plan! Make lists! Figure out in advance for the first time in college history what everybody's supposed to do."

He went on down the list of things to be done, leaving nothing and nobody out. Enthusiasm ran so high that he had to yell, "Shut up!" a few more times, but he did so in a jovially paternal way. The concept that they had been victims of a heinous plot, that they would triumph over every obstacle and show those crummy saboteurs where to get off, was firing their blood as mere exhortation could never have done. When he concluded with, "And now we need eight volunteers to ride our horses out to Forgery Point tonight," every man and woman in the bleachers, not excepting Matilda Gables, rose and surged forward.

Swiftly, knowing exactly who could spare the time and who could stick on the back of a saddleless horse over several miles of bad road, Svenson selected his riders. All were sensible, reliable plodders who would be unlikely to distinguish themselves in competition and thus were given an unexpected chance to reap their kudos in advance. One Henry Purvis, a lackluster wight who couldn't ride, couldn't plow, couldn't whang a drum, couldn't do much of anything except scrape through his classwork and handle any vehicle from a minibike to a bulldozer the way the late Serge Koussevitzky handled a baton, was given the proud task of driving the van that was to carry the harness, nudge along the stragglers, and fetch home the riders after the horses had been delivered to the smithy.

"Who gets to drive the wagon to the fairgrounds?" yelled somebody.

"I do," said Svenson. "Dismissed."

"But what if you're hijacked?" The questioner persisted.

"Urrgh!" the President replied, and nobody could doubt that he meant it.

Chapter 20

Shandy ought then to have gone home for breakfast. Helen would be wondering where he'd gone and what he was doing. However, for the first time since he'd laid eyes on Helen Marsh at the airport, he preferred to keep away from her. He called the house from a campus phone.

"I'm up here with the President. We've had another general assembly to get organized for the Competition. It's all hands to the pumps. I don't know when or whether I'll be able to get home. If I don't show up, could you throw a change of clothes in the car and meet me at the fairgrounds tomorrow morning?"

"Peter, are you up to something?" was Helen's answer, as he might have known it would be.

"Right now I've got to ride out to Forgery Point and see how Flackley's getting on with the wagon," he replied evasively but truthfully. "I may have to stick around and give him a hand."

"Have you eaten anything?"

"As a matter of fact," he lied, "I'm calling from the faculty dining room. Will it inconvenience you if I use our car, or shall I try to borrow the President's?"

"For Heaven's sake, not Thorkjeld's! You know he holds that wreck together only by sheer force of will. Iduna and I can always thumb a ride with Grace Porble if we have to. Drive ours by all means. At least I shan't have to worry about the wheels falling off."

"Helen, you don't have to worry about anything," he

protested. "Just—er—stick with Charlotte Brontë. Lots of good stuff in there."

He hung up quickly. After all, it mightn't be a bad idea to get something at the dining room. He hadn't been throwing much business that way lately.

Mrs. Mouzouka herself, head of the cookery department, came to take his order. "Morning, Professor. All my helpers are grooming horses or pressing uniforms, so you'll have to make do with poor service and scant choice. Mrs. Svenson was down helping me yesterday, but today I expect she'll be busy braiding manes and tails."

Getting the Balaclava Blacks ready for the Competition involved elaborate hairdressing. Nobody had ever been able to emulate Sieglinde Svenson's touch with horsehair.

Shandy had an inspiration. "I'll take whatever you have, and perhaps I can volunteer my wife. She and her friend Miss Bjorklund have been running a sort of amateur breadline for the pig hunters, but I shouldn't think they'd have any customers today."

He ate the scrambled eggs and hot cornbread his colleague brought him, then made a second call. "Helen, do you suppose you and Iduna could pitch in here for a while? Mrs. Mouzouka's trying to run the dining room virtually single-handed."

Helen said of course they'd be glad to, and Shandy hung up feeling smug. That should give them plenty to do and keep their minds off other things. He got the car and headed for Forgery Point.

Flackley certainly looked as though he'd been working all night, and so did the wagon. Repairs were well along.

"Well, I see we're going to make it," was Shandy's greeting.

"Oh yeah, no sweat."

The smith rubbed a blackened arm over his moist forehead. " 'Cept mine, that is. Mind holding the whiffletree while I attach these here fittings?"

"Not at all. I'm relieved to see you found some. The old fittings were broken, weren't they?"

"Smashed all to hell an' gone," Flackley grunted. "I practically had to make these over, but— Ah, now she fits! Smooth as a kitten's wrist. Hold'er steady, can't you?"

He tinkered awhile, then ordered, "Okay, let'er go easy. Easy, for God's sake! If them things snap off—

Nope, guess they're goin' to hold. Okay, Professor, looks like you c'n go back and tell'em she'll be ready to roll by the time you get them horses out here. Eight o'clock, you said?"

"Give or take half an hour. We'll let them amble along at their own pace."

"Thass ri', do' wanna tire'em out."

Flackley was speaking indistinctly now since he'd put a number of screws into his mouth and gone on to another job. Shandy began to feel his presence redundant, at least in the blacksmith's opinion. Still he lingered, wandering around the wagon, checking a repair here or there, making approving comments on Flackley's skill. He himself had cobbled together enough broken farm equipment to recognize exactly what Flackley was doing and how well the man was doing it. At last he clambered up into the dray.

"I see you've got all the barrels screwed back down." He reached out to twist one in its flange.

Flackley spat out screws. "For Chrissakes," he yelled, "don't touch'em. I spent three, four hours puttin' them staves back together like a jigsaw puzzle. Couldn't find nothin' but that old-fashioned slow-dryin' glue and she ain't had time to set yet. Look, Professor, you want to do me a great, big favor?"

"And get the hell out of here?" Shandy finished for him cheerfully. "Sure. I'll mosey along and break the joyful tidings. I think I'll also take a little cruise along the old county road as far as the fairgrounds, in case there might be any bad potholes to look out for. They won't let us take the wagon out on the main highway, you know."

"Yeah," mumbled Flackley around another mouthful of screws. "That's a great idea. See you later."

"The later the better, eh?" Shandy headed for his car. "Thanks, Flackley, you've taken a big load off my mind."

He drove back out to the Seven Forks, stopped at the noisome general store, and used its pay phone to let Miss Tibbett at the college administration building know things were under control at the forge and ask her to spread the word. Then he began a slow, thoughtful progress of the narrow, twisting, ill-paved route over which the wagon would be traveling that night. At several points he stopped the car, got out, and made careful exploration, taking his time, keeping his eyes peeled and his mind on his job.

At last he nodded, stepped on the gas, and headed for home.

He managed to locate Lieutenant Corbin and had a long, earnest talk with the state policeman. Then he put his car away because he wouldn't be needing it again, went back to the Crescent, and found his house deserted. Helen and Iduna must still be putting their shoulders to the wheel up at the faculty dining room.

That suited him fine. He ate a sandwich that had been thoughtfully left for him in a Baggie on the kitchen table, drank a glass of milk, and took a nap. At a quarter to five he woke up, took a shower, put on fresh underwear, and topped it with the most villainously tattered work shirt and pants he possessed. He packed some less disreputable garments into a canvas carryall, put on his old mackinaw, and walked to the faculty dining room.

Helen was waitressing for all she was worth. Though she set a plate of rolls and a glass of water in front of him with professional flair, her greeting was that of any loving wife.

"Peter, couldn't you find anything else to put on?"

"I have a change with me."

He showed her the canvas bag. "I wore this rig because I'll probably have to help unharness and then sleep in the wagon at the fairgrounds."

"Oh, then you're going to the fairgrounds?"

"Yes, Thorkjeld and I. The students will come by bus. That way there's less chance of a breakdown, though Flackley seems to have the repairs well in hand. What's for supper?"

"Iduna made the most elegant beef stew."

"Good. Trot it out."

In due time, Helen was back with a brimming plateful. *"Bon appétit.* It's on the house. Mrs. Mouzouka's so grateful to you for sending Iduna that she'd come and kiss you if she didn't have her hands in a batch of piecrust. They're swapping recipes like mad, and I have a hunch she's warming up to offer Iduna a job."

"Say, that might be just the ticket! Iduna could move over with Tim and—"

"Yes, dear."

Helen dropped a kiss on his left ear and went off to serve another table. Shandy finished his stew, ate a double helping of apple pie and ice cream, drank more coffee than he normally would at this hour, shoved a quarter under the plate, managed to snatch a good-bye kiss as Helen whizzed past with a trayful of dishes, and headed for the barns.

Here, all was in readiness. The eight magnificent Balaclava Blacks were lined up outside their stalls, their coats a-glisten, their manes and tails exquisitely coiffed, their hooves polished, their eyes steadfast and resolute.

The eight bareback riders, smartly togged out in clean dungarees and their best J. C. Penney flannel shirts, were ready to mount. The harness had been loaded into the minibus, behind whose steering wheel sat the once lackluster Henry Purvis, the cynosure of all eyes and the envy of a good many hearts.

Thorkjeld Svenson was stomping up and down the line giving last-minute instructions. Jim Feldster was much in evidence, carrying a huge checklist, looking solemn and responsible. He appeared to be doing a fairly good impersonation of Stott, already savoring the position of head man in charge at the animal husbandry department. Shandy eyed him reflectively for a moment, then got into the minibus and stuck his satchel under the seat behind Purvis.

As if that had been the signal they were waiting for, although in fact it was not, the eight riders swung up on their mounts and took the reins in hand. The Balaclava Boosters' Drum and Bugle Band, lined up in full uniform, began a campus favorite, and the vast crowd took up the strain:

"When the farmer comes to town, with his wagon broken down,
"Oh, the farmer is the man that beats'em all!"

Thorkjeld Svenson stepped to the head of the line, clucked softly into Odin's ear, and the greatest of all those great horses put his best foot forward. Henry Purvis started idling his engine. Shandy looked out at the cheering crowd and went back to sleep.

When he woke, Thorkjeld Svenson was beside him and they were bumping over that dirt road he'd got to know so well during the past couple of days. "Almost there," he grunted.

"Hope Flackley's ready for us," Svenson grunted back. "He damn well better be."

He was. Flackley had rigged a floodlight outside the smithy, and they could see the wagon standing there, looking rugged and sturdy as ever. Svenson and Shandy checked it over, tested everything testable, and could see no cause for worry.

"I screwed them barrels in as tight as I could," said the farrier, "and I'm sure that glue'll be set by morning. Just go easy on'em tonight. Them guys on the horses ain't ridin' with you, are they?"

"No," Shandy assured him. "They're just going to help us harness up, then go back in the bus with our man Purvis, there. It'll be just President Svenson and myself in the wagon tonight, unless you'd care to join us for the ride."

Flackley grinned. "Not me, thanks. I'm gonna catch up on a little sack time right here, where it's nice an' comfortable. I'll be over to the fairgrounds at daybreak tomorrow, though, in case there's any last-minute problem."

Svenson engulfed the farrier's hand in a mighty paw. "Damned grateful. Give you an honorary degree, maybe."

"Thanks, I'll settle for cash. You folks want me to help harness up? If not, I think I'll get me some grub. Can't remember when I et last."

"Go ahead. We'll manage."

Svenson and his crew began dragging out the harness and hitching the horses in tandem: Odin and Thor leading with battery lanterns hung about their necks, then Freya and Balder, then Hoenir and Heimdallr, with Loki and Tyr bringing up the rear. When the team was ready to roll, the riders got into the minibus, each with a personal handshake and a word of commendation from the President which he or she would treasure forever.

Henry Purvis came in for well-deserved encomiums. He was all for seeing the wagon safely out to the fairgrounds, but Svenson pointed out in a fatherly tone that his first obligation was to his passengers, that they'd be late enough getting to bed as it was, and that Balaclava expected every bus driver to do his duty. With those words ringing in his ears, Purvis saluted smartly, turned the bus with the ease of Nureyev doing a pirouette, and in a moment the red taillight went bobbing down the rutted lane.

That left Svenson and Shandy alone with the team. As they began their long, lonely ride, they could observe Flackley through the lighted kitchen window, opening a can of chili.

Neither of the two on the wagon seat felt like talking. Shandy wasn't sleepy anymore, though. He had an odd feeling that he wasn't even there, that he was somewhere outside, watching to see what was going to happen to that balding little chap in the torn work pants and the giant who hulked beside him.

Well, he'd done all he could to get ready. Now there was nothing to do but wait. He expected he and Svenson would be waiting quite a while, and he was right.

It happened exactly where he'd thought it would, almost at the end of the old road, in the little dip where the abandoned tannery stood. They came without a sound, three of them, bandannas masking their faces. One rushed out from the shadows and grabbed Odin's traces. The other two jumped into the wagon from the roof of the low deserted building.

They didn't have guns; Shandy hadn't thought they would. They'd have been crazy to risk shots so close to the main highway, with a police blockade stationed at the crossroad. They were carrying blackjacks. They might as well have relied on peashooters.

Thorkjeld Svenson took a mighty blow to the back of his skull without even wincing, turned on the man who'd delivered it, grabbed him by the feet, swung him around a few times, and whacked his head against the wagon seat. At the same moment Shandy, who'd been crouching behind one of the band seats, leaped on the other man, brought him down, ripped off his bandanna, and used it to tie his hands behind his back, almost in one motion.

The man on the ground, seeing what was happening, let go of Odin and tried to run for it. Shandy yelled, "Stop!" Svenson didn't say anything. He simply reached for one of the beer kegs, wrenched it from the floor, flange and all, and heaved the missile at the moving figure. The barrel fell short, scattering hoops and staves in all directions, but one of those flying hoops neatly lassoed the quarry and brought him crashing.

"Yesus, that thing was heavy," the President panted. "What did Flackley do, fill'em with concrete?"

"Not concrete, President," said Shandy, who was now tying up the man Svenson had knocked cold. "It was probably gold, and it belongs to the Carlovingian Crafters. And these are the bastards who took it. Stay here and bop either one who moves a finger. I'll go hobble that third crook before he manages to untangle himself. I don't know what in hell's keeping our escort."

At that moment a police car hauled up behind them. Lieutenant Corbin and Sergeant Lubbock rushed toward the wagon, guns drawn.

"Sorry, gentlemen," said Shandy, "I'm afraid you're too late for the entertainment, but you're welcome to the leftovers. Here's one festooned with a barrel hoop, and two more tied up in the wagon."

"But we were right behind you," stammered young Lubbock.

"Yes, well—er—sorry, things happened rather fast. They were counting on catching us by surprise, of course, and they were under the further handicap of never having seen President Svenson when he's—er—annoyed."

"Damned disappointing," said Svenson morosely. "Bunch of pantywaists. I was looking forward to a little workout to relieve the monotony. Well, let's get this goddamn gold and silver out of the wagon and move on before Odin's legs stiffen up. I suppose all the kegs are full."

"Oh yes," Shandy replied. "I'm sure they are. He and his accomplices must have got to work as soon as you and I left Forgery Point yesterday. That's why he killed Miss Flackley, of course, so that he could get the use of the old forge. He vandalized our wagon so that he could maneuver us into letting him keep it at the smithy long enough to melt down the metal and fill those thirty-six beer kegs. He must have thought he'd found a foolproof way to run your very efficient roadblock, Lieutenant."

Shandy put out a boot and rolled over the man whom Svenson had knocked on the head. The face thus revealed was not unhandsome, but the words that came out of Frank Flackley's mouth as he regained consciousness were very, very ugly.

Chapter 21

Corbin's radioed request for a paddy wagon and an armored truck were received with skepticism at police headquarters until he explained why he needed them. Then he got action fast. Within an hour, the three prisoners were booked and the thirty-six beer kegs full of gold and silver started on the journey that would ultimately take them back to the Carlovingian Crafters' strong room.

The Balaclava Blacks were on the move again, but Peter Shandy was not with them. In his place, Thorkjeld had an escort of two strapping state policemen whom he entertained by singing "I'm an Old Cowhand" in Swedish. They reached the fairgrounds without further incident. Sometime later, the *Balaclava County Weekly Fane and Pennon* published a curious bit of rural folklore about a demon wagoneer who is alleged to go rushing along the old county road howling an uncouth melody no human throat could produce, driving a team of eight coal-black horses, each of them, as the oldest Svenson girl's husband would doubtless have put it, bigger than all the rest.

Having formally identified Flackley's two assistant hooligans as the men who held his wife hostage at gunpoint and forced him and Mr. Peaslee to loot the strong room, Shandy hitched a ride with Sergeant Lubbock back to the Crescent. Helen must have been wakeful, for she heard him come in, and called down.

"Peter, is that you?"

"Yes, my love. Arise and meet the joyous morn."

"It isn't morn, it's only a quarter to two. What's the matter? Did the wagon break down?"

"*Au contraire,* as we say at the Sûreté. Come on, wake up Iduna and tell her to take out her curl papers."

"Peter, are you by any chance drunk?"

"Not by chance, but I may be on purpose before long. Hurry up, put some clothes on."

"What sort of clothes?"

"Any sort. We shan't be going far."

"Where are we going, for goodness' sake?"

"Yonder. If you two ladies would get a move on, I should be able to fill you in on recent events before he gets here."

"He who?"

"Guess."

"Peter, you are exasperating!"

Exasperation served its purpose. The two women were soon downstairs, Helen in slacks and pullover, Iduna wearing an embroidered dirndl that made her look not only immense but also immensely adorable. Her first words to Peter were, "Want me to put the coffee on?"

"By all means," said Shandy. "Make plenty. Better trot out some doughnuts, too."

"How many?"

"Oh, just open the crock."

"Peter," gasped Helen, "you don't mean—"

"I am rife with meaning."

"But how?"

"All will be revealed. Haul up and set, ladies. I would a tale unfold."

And unfold he did. After a brief rundown of the night's action, he proceeded to elucidate.

"As you know, the puzzler about that Carlovingian Crafters robbery was, what happened to all that gold and silver? It made, as we have painful cause to know, a large and heavy load. Ergo, a large and heavy vehicle was required to transport it. The two men who committed the crime were seen and described to a fare-thee-well. Within fifteen minutes the police were throwing up road-blocks from hell to breakfast, stopping and searching all possibly suspect vehicles. Yet they found nothing, and the reason was that the men who stole it didn't try to get away with it.

"Frank Flackley was waiting nearby in a car driven by yet a fourth person. They were concealed on one of those disused logging roads, but not a cul-de-sac like the one you were found on, Helen. There used to be a whole network of such roads around the area, and the criminals had taken great pains to scout out a few that were still viable.

"You and one of the two men were transferred to the other car, which drove off, dropped you where you'd have a reasonably difficult time finding help, and proceeded boldly down the highway to some point or other where the second man was dropped off. Since nobody had seen the second car in connection with the robbers, there was no need for its driver to hide.

"In the meantime, Flackley and the first man drove the van to Forgery Point via those old roads, reached the smithy without being seen, and unloaded the loot. They didn't have to hurry. Flackley had seen his aunt's schedule for the day and knew how long she'd be away. He also knew it was perfectly safe to hide the gold and silver close to the forge because she'd never get to see it. She was going out to dinner and she wasn't coming back.

"The first man, having changed clothes at Flackley's, drove the van to where Matilda Gables found it and torched it to destroy any possible fingerprints or other clues. He then departed on foot, probably disguised as a hiker or jogger so he wouldn't look out of place trotting along the highway. Anyway, he didn't go far away. Flackley, of course, stayed put. When Aunt Martha came home, she no doubt found him parked in front of the TV swilling beer and gassing about how much he'd enjoyed a restful day after his long bus ride the day before."

"Then which of them killed Miss Flackley?" Helen demanded.

"Flackley, of course. After he'd complimented his aunt on her gown and whatnot, I expect he strolled out ostensibly to wave bye-bye and yell, 'Have fun,' or whatever, then pretended to go back to the house. In fact, he swung himself inside the back of the van and stayed there all the time she was with us. After she'd said good night to Stott and was leaving the parking lot, Flackley simply reached from behind, slit her throat right through that mohair stole she was wearing, then took the wheel. He no doubt gave the stole an extra turn or two around her neck so that the blood wouldn't spurt all over the cab, and drove up to the college barns, where he dumped her into the mash hopper."

"And then he stole Belinda," cried Iduna. "But where did he take her? How did he get her in and out of that van all by himself?"

"I'll get to that shortly. As you must already have gathered, stealing the pig and all that folderol with pork chops and pigs' feet and sunflower seeds strewn around the van was camouflage, to make the whole business look like a student prank that had gone wrong and throw us off the track. Which I have to admit it did, for a while."

"But how on earth did Flackley manage to be in so many places at once?" said Helen. "That's what's been puzzling Iduna and me. We knew the minute he opened his mouth, of course, that he wasn't quite what he pretended to be."

"You did? How?"

"His kind never is," Iduna replied for her. "There's a certain type of man who wouldn't tell you the straight truth if you paid him by the word. Helen and I have both got the old snake-oil treatment often enough to know when somebody's pouring it on."

"Then why didn't you tell me?"

"Peter darling," Helen expostulated, "being a liar doesn't necessarily make one a thief and a murderer. We thought Flackley was probably just trying to make a little time with Iduna. We didn't stop him because we wanted to find out if there was anything more to it than that before we started spreading tales about the man. It was only fair."

"And besides, he had that sexy, smoldering quality," snarled her husband. "I hope that'll be a lesson to you."

"My stars," said Iduna, "I hope you don't think either of us would ever have touched him with a ten-foot pole. Not when we could have the company of fine, intellectual gentlemen like you and—and some of the other professors I've—"

Her voice dwindled to a sigh. Shandy glanced at her interestedly, then resumed his narrative.

"Vandalizing our wagon was easy for a man who must really have had the sort of experience Flackley claimed he did. In fact, he did it much too well for credibility. He'd obviously taken inventory at the smithy, knew what replacement parts were available, and smashed the pieces that would be easy for a blacksmith with the right equipment to fix. A real vandal wouldn't have gone for the metal as he did, but would have demolished the seats, perhaps set fire to the wooden body, knocked the spokes out of the wheels, things like that.

"Flackley did knock out a few hoops and staves, but he did it in such a way that the barrels could easily be made usable again. Once I'd seen the sort of damage that was done and remembered how adroitly he'd let us know he was an expert wagon-fixer, I finally got it through my thick skull that we'd been very neatly conned. I knew I could put the wagon right myself in a few hours, given the tools and parts, so when he made his big hoopla about its being an all-night job, I realized he must be planning to melt down the metal and pour it into the kegs. After that, the best thing to do was let the scheme go on and—er—catch them gold-handed."

"Peter Shandy," gasped his wife, "do you mean you knew those men were going to attack the wagon, and you deliberately let yourself and Thorkjeld be sitting ducks? What if they'd shot you?"

"My love, we were not sitting ducks. In the first place, Thorkjeld knew what was going to happen, and was looking forward to the experience with considerable zest. In the second place, he and I were both wearing bulletproof vests and helmets lent us by Lieutenant Corbin, who was right on our tails in a police cruiser. In the third place, I was pretty sure there wouldn't be any shooting, and there wasn't. Flackley and his gang expected to have the jump on us, you see. They were carrying blackjacks, which simply bounced off our helmets."

"Seems kind of complicated to me," said Iduna. "Why'd they have to go through all that rigmarole?"

"Because they had to get the gold and silver past the police roadblocks. On that route, the one ticklish point was where the old county road joins the main highway. Almost any other large vehicle would have been stopped and searched, but they knew the police wouldn't interfere with the Balaclava wagon. It would be like arresting the Bunker Hill Monument. We'd be expected to cross there at just about that time, you see, and that's what would happen, only somebody else would be driving.

"I reasoned that Flackley and his lads would delay the attack as long as they could, rather than risk the chance that some of our students might ride out to escort us part of the way and find out the wagon had been hijacked. However, they couldn't wait till we'd got across the highway because then we'd be on the fairgrounds road. Other teams would be coming along, and they might either be spotted or jump the wrong team in the dark and blow the whole performance. I scouted the route yesterday and decided they'd be most apt to pull their ambush from that old tannery next to the road, about a quarter of a mile from the crossing."

"And that, I assume, is where they were," said Helen. "Darn you, Peter, you make it sound so—so easy!"

"Well, it was, when you come right down to it. The hardest part was the waiting."

"But did they actually intend to drive our wagon all the way to the fairgrounds? How would they have got the barrels away?"

"With ease and finesse. One of the crooks drives for a brewery in his—er—more legitimate moments. His truck was parked out behind the tannery. He'd have driven it out to the highway right in front of the wagon. He knew he'd be stopped and searched, and he wanted to be. That would keep the police busy, and they'd be even more apt to wave the wagon across.

"The driver would have explained that he was headed for the fairgrounds to supply the refreshment stand with beer for the Competition. The police would slosh all the barrels around, maybe tap a few to make sure it really was beer, which of course it was, then they'd let him through. He'd tootle on up to the fairgrounds as advertised, then he and his cohorts would switch his barrels for ours, pile into the truck with the loot, and hightail it for God knows where. Sooner or later, our bugle boys would have realized they were sitting on full kegs instead of empties, but by then Flackley and the rest would be long gone."

"You mean that fuzzy-faced rodeo hand planned the whole stunt?" said Iduna. "I can't believe it."

"I'm not asking you to. Flackley's no planner. He's not even a hundred percent perfect at doing what he's told. For instance, he was rather careless when he burned Miss Flackley's mohair stole out at the old forge. I found some bits of brown fuzz among the ashes while I was wandering around making a nuisance of myself there yesterday."

"Then who—"

A County Seat Taxi stopped in front of the house. A very large man got out.

"Ah," said Shandy, "here he comes now."

"Professor Stott! Peter, you can't mean—"

"Perish the thought. Our tale is not yet told. Ah, Stott, old friend, come in. Come in!"

"Shandy, my trusty comrade!"

The colleagues wrung hands. Even as he thanked the man who'd got him free, however, Stott's eyes were elsewhere.

"Good evening, Miss Bjorklund. The prodigal, as you see, returns."

Iduna gave him a three-hundred-candlepower smile, then dropped her eyes demurely. "Want some coffee?" she murmured.

"Later," Shandy barked. "Grab your coats."

"Peter Shandy," Helen protested, "I refuse to budge till you tell us where we're going."

"There, naturally." He pointed directly across the Crescent.

"To Tim's house? Whatever for?"

"Because, damn it."

Shandy grabbed his wife's elbow and hustled her over the green. Ames's front door was standing ajar. He pushed it wide open, switched on a light, and beckoned them inside.

"Whew," gasped Iduna. "A person could choke to death in here."

"A person was intended to," Shandy replied, "so that another person could gain time for a quiet getaway. Better leave that door open. Fortunately, Tim was on the alert and bopped that she-devil over the head with a bottle of Lysol while she was mixing him a bucketful of ammonia and bleach water as a farewell present."

"Lorene McSpee!"

"None other. She wangled herself a job here, snooped around and gathered local gossip from Mirelle Feldster, searched out escape routes in Tim's car while she was supposedly off buying more bleach water, laid her plans, lined up two confederates, then sent for Flackley. They did the real work while she took care of the odd jobs,

like making those funny phone calls, planting the pigs'
feet and pork chops, and scattering sunflower seeds
around to confuse the issue. By the way, her blood's
Type O, and she does have a nasty abrasion on one
finger."

"I'll bet she did that switching the horseshoes around,"
said Helen, "and I'm afraid I was the one who gave her
the idea. I mentioned that discussion I'd had about horseshoes with Miss Flackley and Professor Stott the night she
came to dinner."

"As her boyfriend the blacksmith would say, don't
sweat it. Her own luck ran out, not ours. I'm delighted
to inform you that Lorene McSpee is now in the steel
château, charged with conspiracy, attempted murder, and
grand larceny."

"Peter, how lovely! How could they charge her with
grand larceny, though? She didn't actually take part in
the robbery, did she?"

"She drove the car they transferred you to. Don't
forget, however, that there was more than one robbery,
and more to her bleach water than met the nose."

He led them to the cellar door and threw it open. On
the top step sat Timothy Ames, armed to the teeth with a
coal shovel and a pair of hedge clippers. Feeling the
draft, Ames whirled to attack.

"Move one step closer and I'll whang the daylights
out of—Oh, hi, Pete. What the hell took you so long?"

"I was waiting for Stott. It would have been a shame
for him to miss the joyful reunion."

"Reunion?"

With a jubilant cry, Stott hurtled down the stairs. A
frenzied oinking filled the air.

"Perhaps we ought to leave them alone together,"
Helen murmured. "Peter, how did you ever guess she
was here?"

"You told me, my love, you and the Brontë sisters.
Your little japery about the apprentice keeping the books
under his bed set me thinking. What if Belinda never did
go anywhere in that van? What if she'd simply trotted
somewhere on her own four feet, lured by a bucketful of
succulent swill, or whatever, while the droppings were
planted as camouflage?

"Then I got to wondering where she might be, and it

hit me in the face like a gallon of Lysol that there might
be a good reason why a woman would keep a house
reeking of disinfectant. The McSpee creature had been—
er—building up an atmosphere, as it were. It made sense.
Tim never goes into his own cellar. In fact, she'd got him
so terrorized he's been staying away from the house altogether as much as possible. Also, being deaf, he wouldn't
be apt to hear Belinda if she squealed, though I expect
she was kept tranquillized much of the time. So I came
over and looked, and here she was, living on kennel
chow left over from that time Jemima took a notion
to breed grayhounds. I alerted Tim, and he rose nobly
to the cause. By George, Iduna, I told you Timothy
Ames was a great man in a pinch, and—"

"Don't waste your breath," Helen interrupted *sotto
voce*.

Professor Stott was no longer scratching Belinda's back.
He was standing stock-still, gazing upward as Sir Percival
might have gazed upon the Holy Grail.

"Miss Bjorklund," he said tenderly, "may I have the
ineffable pleasure of presenting Belinda of Balaclava?"

"The pleasure is all mine."

Iduna hastened to the bottom of the stairs. At once,
Belinda waddled over and offered her back to be scratched.
It was a beautiful moment, till Timothy Ames spoiled it.

"How the bloody flaming hell," he demanded testily,
"are we going to get that damned great tub of lard out
of my cellar?"

"Open the bulkhead," said Iduna. "I'll get her out."

Stott hastened to do his lady's bidding. Light as a
fairy taking off from a pussywillow, she tripped up the
two steps and stood just outside. Her honeyed voice
soared from a beguiling *pianissimo* to a rich *mezzo forte*:

"Soo-ee. Soo-ee! Peeeg! Pig! Pig!"

Belinda cocked an ear, turned her roseate snout toward the open bulkhead, then, as though drawn by an
invisible cord, began climbing the steps toward that
siren call. So did Professor Stott.

"Miss Bjorklund," he echoed, "That—that was the
most eloquent—the most superb—the—the most—"

"Oh," she whispered, "why don't you just call me
Iduna?"

'Iduna!" he breathed softly. Then with fervor, "Iduna!
My—my own given name is Daniel."

"There, now! I knew it would be something distinguished and high-minded. Well, Daniel, what do you say you and I walk Belinda back to her pen, then you drop over to the house for a bite of breakfast?"

Hand in hand, with Belinda waddling contentedly behind them, they strolled into the sunrise.

Junction Jottings

By Arabella Goulson

Readers will be glad to know that the recent happenings at Balaclava Agricultural College (Ed. Note: See pages 1,5,6, and 8 for complete details) didn't throw our team off its stride at the Annual Draft Horse Competition. (Ed. Note: See pages 1,2,3,4, and 7 for complete details.)

As usual, President Thorkjeld Svenson captured the Senior Plowmen's Trophy, and this year popular man-about-campus Hjalmar Olafssen managed to wrest first place in the Juniors' event from former champion Ethelred Spinney of Lumpkin Corners. Too bad, Eth, but a little bird tells us there was more than a silver cup waiting for Hjalmar at the end of that furrow.

Special congratulations are due to dark horse Henry Purvis, who earned a surprising third in the Horseshoe Pitch, right up there with such experts as Oscar Plantagenet of West Lumpkinville and Walt Hayward of Goat Valley. Keep an eye on Henry next year, folks! Jennifer Berg and Alison Blair won all hearts and a Tricolor Award with their daredevil stunt riding on Freya and Balder.

Only fly in our local ointment was that the Balaclava Boosters' Drum and Bugle Band had to play standing up in our historic wagon during the opening procession since their seats, if you'll pardon the levity, had been pinched. (Ed. Note: See page 1 for special feature story.) Nice footwork, bandspersons! We're sorry about that bass drum, but you can't win 'em all, Hjalmar.

BALACLAVA COUNTY WEEKLY FANE AND PENNON, May 11
Junction Jottings
By Arabella Goulson

Readers will be interested to know that Miss Iduna Bjorklund of Bjorklund's Bend, South Dakota, who has been visiting Professor and Mrs. Peter Shandy of the Crescent, has been offered a position at the college. She will serve as special assistant and consultant to Mrs. Blanche Mouzouka, head of the Cookery Department.

Rumor hath it that Miss Bjorklund may soon be offered another position, perchance in the Animal Husbandry Department? Who was that lovely lady we saw you waltzing so divinely with at the Seniors' Ball, Professor S?

By the way, we're thrilled to report that Belinda of Balaclava (Ed. Note: See *Agricultural Happenings,* page 2, for complete details) has given birth to no fewer than seventeen prime piglets. We all knew you had it in you, Belinda! Mother and babies are doing fine.

BALACLAVA COUNTY WEEKLY FANE AND PENNON, June 22
Junction Jottings
By Arabella Goulson

Readers would have been as charmed as hubby Harry and Your Humble Correspondent were by the beautiful tea which President and Mrs. Thorkjeld Svenson gave on Sunday afternoon to announce the engagement of their daughter Birgit to Mr. Hjalmar Olafssen of Buckbury Lower Falls and to celebrate the recent marriage of Professor Daniel Stott to the former Miss Iduna Bjorklund. (Ed. Note: See *Society,* page 6, for complete details.)

Pink-covered tables dotted the lush green lawns of the Svensons' gracious home on Valhalla like giant roses, each with a cute centerpiece of bachelor's buttons and hollyhock ladies fashioned by the clever fingers of Mrs. Philip Porble, wife of the College Librarian and chairman of the Garden Club's Horticultural Committee. We're so proud of our talented Grace!

To everyone's delight and astonishment, as we partook of a delicious smorgasbord prepared by Mrs. Sieglinde Svenson and her lovely daughters, President Svenson raised his champagne glass and announced that this was—surprise!—a triple celebration. It was his great pleasure to announce that Royall Ames, Class of '75 and only son of the distinguished Professor Timothy Ames of the Soil Management Department has returned from his exciting trip to Antarctica, bringing with him a charming bride!

She's the former Miss Laurie Jilles of Downer's Grove, Illinois, who was also a member of the expedition. They were married smack in the middle of the Ross Sea by Captain Amos Flackley, leader of the expedition. Asked if they planned a return to South Polar regions, Roy whispered in Your Demon Reporter's ear that he and Laurie have both been offered teaching fellowships right here at Balaclava and will be making their home with Dr. Ames at the Crescent. Thanks for the scoop, Roy!

By the way, Captain Flackley sends his sincere apologies to all his family's old customers in Balaclava County. Seems he didn't hear of his aunt's sad demise and the outrageous impersonation by Ferdinand McSpee, who pretended to be a member of the family and was in fact a former maintenance man at the Carlovingian Crafters, among other things!! (Ed. Note: McSpee, alias Frank Flackley, has been arraigned on a charge of murder and grand larceny. See complete details page 4.)

Captain Flackley asked Roy to tell us that he will be back at the Forgery Point smithy, ready for business, as soon as he puts the finishing touches to a documentary film of his Antarctic expedition and finds a good home for a pair of very well-behaved Adelie penguins. Hang in there, horse lovers!

And here's a final tidbit for all you folklore enthusiasts. According to the erudite Dr. Thorkjeld Svenson, Iduna was the Scandinavian goddess of youth and springtime. She kept the golden apples which the gods ate to preserve their eternal youth. Hubby Harry says jokingly that having an Iduna around town sounds bad for his business, but some of us gals in the Garden Club could sure use a few hints on growing those golden apples. How about it, Mrs. Stott?